MONSTERS
IN THE
MIST

The Mystery of Entity 303 series

Books by Mark Cheverton

The Gameknight999 Series
Invasion of the Overworld
Battle for the Nether
Confronting the Dragon

The Mystery of Herobrine Series: A Gameknight999 Adventure
Trouble in Zombie-town
The Jungle Temple Oracle
Last Stand on the Ocean Shore

Herobrine Reborn Series: A Gameknight999 Adventure
Saving Crafter
The Destruction of the Overworld
Gameknight999 vs. Herobrine

Herobrine's Revenge Series: A Gameknight999 Adventure
The Phantom Virus
Overworld in Flames
System Overload

The Birth of Herobrine: A Gameknight999 Adventure
The Great Zombie Invasion
Attack of the Shadow-Crafters
Herobrine's War

The Mystery of Entity303: A Gameknight999 Adventure
Terrors of the Forest
Monsters in the Mist
Mission to the Moon (Coming Soon!)

The Gameknight999 Box Set
The Gameknight999 vs. Herobrine Box Set
The Gameknight999 Adventures Through Time Box Set (Coming Soon!)

The Rise of the Warlords: An Unofficial Interactive Minecrafter's Adventure
Zombies Attack! (Coming Soon)
The Bones of Doom (Coming Soon)
Into the Spiders' Lair (Coming Soon!)

The Algae Voices of Azule Series
Algae Voices of Azule
Finding Home
Finding the Lost

AN UNOFFICIAL NOVEL

MONSTERS IN THE MIST

THE MYSTERY OF ENTITY303
BOOK TWO
<<< A GAMEKNIGHT999 ADVENTURE >>>

AN UNOFFICIAL MINECRAFTER'S ADVENTURE

MARK CHEVERTON

SKY PONY PRESS
NEW YORK

Copyright © 2017 by Mark Cheverton

Minecraft® is a registered trademark of Notch Development AB

The Minecraft game is copyright © Mojang AB

Sky Pony Press books may be purchased in bulk at special discounts
for sales promotion, corporate gifts, fund-raising, or educational
purposes. Special editions can also be created to specifications.
For details, contact the Special Sales Department, Sky Pony Press,
307 West 36th Street, 11th Floor, New York, NY 10018 or info@
skyhorsepublishing.com.

Sky Pony® is a registered trademark of Skyhorse Publishing, Inc.®,
a Delaware corporation.

Visit our website at www.skyponypress.com.

10 9 8 7 6 5 4 3 2 1

Library of Congress Cataloging-in-Publication Data is available on file.

Cover design by Owen Corrigan
Cover artwork by Thomas Frick
Technical consultant: Gameknight999

Print ISBN: 978-1-5107-1887-6
Ebook ISBN: 978-1-5107-1890-6

Printed in Canada

ACKNOWLEDGMENTS

To my family, who continue to support my insane writing binges and continual nervousness about getting these books completed on schedule, I say thank you. Without your support and faith in me, I'd never be able to finish any of these books.

To my son, Gameknight999, I have learned so much from you over the last couple of years. Your strength, resilience, and forgiveness are inspirations to me, and maybe one day in the future we will all look back at these days and smile.

To all of my readers, thank you so much for taking my characters into your heart. Your excitement about Gameknight, Crafter, Hunter, Stitcher, Digger and Herder—and of course Tux—has been incredible. Thank you for embracing my books and making them part of your lives.

NOTE FROM THE AUTHOR

As I say every time, this book was the hardest to write, and I wasn't sure if I could get something really good put together for all of you. But now, seeing the finished story, I'm really excited about *Monsters in the Mist*. I hope you'll all enjoy reading it as much as I enjoyed writing it.

To all the young readers who send me emails on my website, www.markcheverton.com, thank you so much for your excitement and kind words. I try to reply to every email, no matter how long or how brief. I love hearing what you think about my books and which one is your favorite. Please keep the emails coming, but make sure you type your own email address correctly so I can reply.

To all the young writers out there, thank you so much for sending me your stories. I love reading about what you create, whether it involves my characters or not. In fact, I don't care if you're writing your own Minecraft-inspired stories, or they're something completely different. It doesn't matter what you write . . . as long as you write. I post everything I receive (as long as it's more than a single sentence) to my website. Cruise through the blog and see all the stories; there are almost 600 there now. If you click on the *FOR TEACHERS* tab, you'll find the writing tutorials I've put together to help young writers with the process of writing. If you find these materials helpful, then share them with your teachers; maybe they can help more kids.

The mod featured in this book, Mystcraft, is incredible, and you can run it a number of ways at home. Search the Internet and you'll find countless recommendations on how you can download it (with your parents' permission, of course). Be sure to check out Direwolf20's Mod Showcase for Mystcraft on YouTube; you'll see how incredible this mod really is. I've added a page to the Gameknight999 website to help you with exploring all the many mods to Minecraft. You can find these instructions and some images here: http://gameknight999.com/modded-minecraft/

We're going to try to add it to the Gameknight999 Server (IP: mc.gameknight999.com), but it has proven difficult in the past. I don't know if we'll be able to get it to work or not. If you are interested in Gameknight's server, go to www.gameknight999.com to see more information. The great server architect and developer, quadbamber, will be adding many new features to the Gameknight999 Network by the time this book is printed, so come online, check it out, and say hi to Gameknight999 and myself, Monkeypants_271.

> Keep reading, keep writing,
> and watch out for creepers.
> Mark

Hating people takes too much energy to sustain. Instead, forgive them, even if you disagree. Learn what the other side thinks, and understand their perspective so that common ground can be found. Forgiveness is a great gift, and by forgiving others, you take hatred out of your life, and out of the lives of others.

CHAPTER 1

DECAYING AGE

The blocky Minecraft world before them was wounded and suffering; with its green sun, blood-red trees and black grass, it looked as if a disease had spread across the land, consuming all that it touched, and then spread upward into the gray sky.

Seconds ago, Gameknight999 and his friends had been in the massive chamber deep under the White Castle in the Twilight Forest mod, but now they stood in this suffering land, shocked by what they saw. They had followed Entity303 into this strange land through the use of a magical book from a mod, Mystcraft, which had been added to Minecraft's servers by Entity303 and had allowed him to avoid capture. Mystcraft gave users the power to create these magical books and use them as gateways into new dimensions, or Ages. And that's what Entity303 had done at the end of their last battle: used a magical book to escape into another dimension, fleeing the Twilight Forest just before being caught by Gameknight999 and his friends. And now, he was somewhere in this strange world.

"Oh, this was a great idea," Hunter said sarcastically, her normally bright red curls looking strangely brown in the light of the emerald sun. "We jump into a magical book and here we are, in a land that looks as if it came out of a nightmare."

"I know this looks confusing, but Entity303 came here for a reason, so we must follow him." Gameknight said as he turned and surveyed the surroundings, a look of horror on his face. "You can see the damage that terrible user has inflicted upon Minecraft. He did something in the past that is ruining everything in the present."

"I only hope this damage can be reversed," Crafter said quietly, his normally bright blue eyes dim and filled with sadness. Though he looked to be the youngest villager in the party, the wise NPC (non-playable character) had lived many lifetimes in Minecraft. "We must hurry and catch this terrible user, Entity303, before it's too late."

Squawk, the penguin, Tux, added.

Stitcher, Hunter's younger sister, reached down and patted the little animal on the head, her bright red curls taking on the same strange, brown luster as her older sister's.

Gameknight glanced at his friends. Normally, their cubic heads, blocky bodies and rectangular arms would have looked artificial, but that had been when he was just playing Minecraft as a game. Now, with his entire *being* actually inside the game—thanks to his father's invention, the Digitizer—there were a million features to each of them. Everything to Gameknight looked real from within the game, and felt real as well; he was really inside the game, but that made all the dangers real as well. He was a user, but really he was more: he was the User-that-is-not-a-user.

"How are we gonna find your little friend, Entity303, anyway?" Hunter asked.

"He's not my little friend," Gameknight snapped, then saw Hunter's grin and relaxed a little, realizing she was joking. "We used the same book he used, so Entity303 should have appeared in this Age, right here, just like we did."

"Well, I don't see him anywhere," Weaver said.

"I'm sure he's here somewhere," Gameknight said. "We have to catch him soon, before he can do more damage. Besides, only Entity303 knows the location of the diamond portal that will send Weaver back home into the past. Everything depends on us getting Weaver back where he belongs."

Young Weaver glared suspiciously at Gameknight999, his blue eyes narrowing.

"You know what I mean," the User-that-is-not-a-user said. "If we don't catch this evil user, then all the damage to Minecraft," he gestured to the surroundings, "cannot be repaired. Catching Entity303 and getting Weaver back into the past so all this damage will never happen is key to Minecraft's survival."

"We know," Stitcher said earnestly. "We're with you, Gameknight . . . we're always with you."

"I know," Gameknight, the User-that-is-not-a-user, replied.

Around them, the black grass stretched in all directions, but ended at the rough edge of the land. In places, the ground was completely missing, as if part of the terrain had just disappeared, somehow. Gameknight999 was about to ask about it when a large hill nearby shuddered for just a moment, throwing a cloud of dust and debris into the air, then fell away, descending into the void. The crashing and grinding of the blocks against each other sounded like some kind of massive, destructive waterfall of stone and dirt. The thunderous noise was deafening.

The party moved closer to the spot where the hill had once stood. Now, a gaping wound replaced the feature, the gash in the ground stretching all the way through the land, leaving an opening that extended down into the terrifying darkness of the void. It exposed the ground beneath the surface of the land, showing only a dozen blocks or so holding up the black grassy blocks and undulating hills. The rest of the stone and dirt that should have been beneath the surface were just gone . . . having already fallen into the darkness.

"This is not good," the tiny gnome, Empech, said grimly. He was from the magical race of Pechs, and had joined the party on their last adventure in the Twilight Forest. "The land suffers, yes, yes. Our enemy must be caught soon, before it is too late."

"What do you mean, 'too late'?" Digger asked. The stocky villager placed Tux on the ground to let the tiny penguin stretch its stubby little legs. "Can this get worse?"

"Yes, yes, much worse," Empech said. "If the fabric of Minecraft is stretched too far, it will tear, as it is doing here. Too many tears and it falls apart, completely."

"That doesn't sound very good," Hunter said.

The gray-skinned pech shook his head. "Minecraft is in great danger, yes, yes."

Suddenly, a group of tiny blue creatures—Gameknight remembered them being called Kobolds—came running toward them, charging out from a collection of small mounds that they now recognized as huts; it was likely their village. They each had spiky white nails at the end of their stubby fingers, and their teeth were sharp and menacing.

"Weren't those things in the Twilight Forest?" Stitcher asked.

"They're called Kobolds," Gameknight explained. "And yes, they were there. All of these mods overlap, so things in the Overworld or in the Twilight Forest will also be here."

"You mean the Hydra might be here?" Digger asked with alarm.

"No, not the bosses, just the monsters."

"Just the monsters?" Hunter asked. "You make that sound so positive."

Gameknight shrugged.

The wolves that guarded the company growled, then moved into a circle, ready to protect the villagers, penguin, gnome and Gameknight999.

"Herder, keep your wolves close," the User-that-is-not-a-user said. "We don't know what's happening here. Everyone else, take out your bows and get ready."

Herder bent and whispered into the ear of the wolf pack leader. The majestic creature then barked a series of commands, causing the twelve wolves to draw into a tight circle around their friends.

Gameknight cast a glance at Digger, then motioned to the little penguin.

Digger nodded. "I'll take care of him," the stocky villager said. He bent down and scooped up Tux, then placed the little animal securely under his arm.

Squawk, Tux protested.

Gameknight smiled, then pulled out his enchanted bow and drew an arrow back, ready to fight.

"Wait, look at their faces," Stitcher said. "They aren't angry, they're afraid."

Suddenly, small meteorites fell from the sky, flames streaming behind the falling stones like fiery tails. They crashed into the ground, exploding in showers of sparks. Many of them plummeted down upon the village, flattening the mounded huts and causing many to burst into flames. With each impact, the ground shook, small earthquakes radiating out from the point of impact. The terrible meteors tore the community apart as if it were made of paper, some crashing down farther away, pounding on the land with a relentless fist.

The ground under the crushed village seemed to lurch to the side, then fell away, the landscape crumbling, falling into the void.

The kobolds, with their large, floppy, elephant-like ears and short stubby legs, ran past the party of NPCs and headed for an opening in the ground. Each wore a tattered brown shirt and equally disheveled shorts, their arms and legs covered with scratches and scars; it was likely they were miners. They streamed down into the dark tunnel, their bright red eyes filled with fear.

Gameknight grabbed one of the creatures; this one wore a nicer vest, its edges lined with gold stitching.

"Tell us, what's happening here?" Gameknight asked.

"Stone tears falling again . . . stone tears falling!" the kobold said in a shrill, difficult-to-understand voice.

"What's going on here?" Crafter asked, putting a hand on the creature's shoulder, hoping to calm him.

The kobold pulled away as if his touch were poison, then turned toward Empech.

"A Third," the creature mumbled. "You must help us. The Third *must* help, it is the law of the Ages."

"What's he talking about?" Crafter asked.

Empech shook his head, a confused look in his blue, crystalline eyes.

"What do you mean?" Gameknight asked the blue monster.

"The world has been crumbling for a while," the monster said, his high-pitched, screechy voice filled with fear. He glanced nervously up to the sky, watching the deadly meteors destroy his world. "It was slow at first, but its speed has been increasing recently. The world will not survive long, . . . My family . . . my friends . . ."

Just then, a gigantic section of the land began to crumble and fall. The kobold watched the land shudder and writhe in pain, then the creature wept for his family and his world.

"Entity303's work, yes, yes," Empech said, a sad expression covering his gray, oversized face "Speed is important. The enemy's trail must be found."

Gameknight glanced at Herder. The lanky boy just shrugged, an angry expression on his square face.

"The wolves can't sense anything other than the acidic smell of this black grass," the lanky boy said.

"Shadow grass, yes, yes," the pech said. "Poisonous stuff."

Gameknight turned back to the kobold. "Did you see a user like me pass through here?"

The little blue monster shook his head, then ducked as a meteor fell nearby, crashing into one of the few red-leafed trees still standing, causing it to burst into flames. Before Gameknight could ask another question, the creature turned and ran for the dark hole that plunged underground, following the rest of his community.

"Wait, stop!" Gameknight shouted, but the creature was already gone.

"Leave him be," Empech said. "That kobold must tend to his people, though there is little that can be done to help the creatures of this world."

In the distance, they saw a huge meteor, the size of a mountain, crash into the landscape. It made the ground quake, causing blocks here and there to crumble into dust.

"Look, there's something over there," Herder shouted, pointing. "A building!"

Gameknight turned and looked where Herder was pointing. Sure enough, the faint outline of a building was just barely visible through the haze of Minecraft.

"It's a library," the User-that-is-not-a-user exclaimed. "There's one of those buildings in every world in Mystcraft. That'll be where Entity303 was heading, I'm sure of it. Come on!"

Gameknight took off in a sprint across the dark grassy plain, the others following close behind. As they ran, the meteor shower grew in intensity, the ground shaking more violently with every impact. No one looked back; they each knew the eventual fate of those poor kobolds, and none of them wanted to see their destruction.

Just then, the land undulated beneath them, throwing all of them to the ground. As Gameknight struggled to stand, he saw a huge section of the terrain, the kobold's tunnel included, shatter into a million blocks and fall into the void. The screams of the poor, doomed creatures were just barely audible over the destruction.

"Come on," Hunter growled determinedly. "Let's keep moving!"

They stood up and continued the race against the meteor shower. Running as fast as they could, the party quickly closed the distance. As they neared the library, all of the features of the structure became visible. The building was made of cobblestone, with a slanted roof and a pair of tall pillars on either side of the door. The library was actually floating on a small island; the endless void wrapped around its edges. A narrow bridge of cobblestone had been hastily built across the gap, allowing them access to the structure.

"Entity303 probably made this bridge to get to the library," Gameknight said, moving up to the edge of the narrow causeway.

One of the wolves sniffed the single-block pathway, then barked and ran across the span.

"Yep, they can smell his scent," Herder said. "Wolves . . . investigate."

The pack of furry white creatures shot across the bridge to check inside and all around the library. The pack leader then emerged from the cobblestone structure and barked once. Herder nodded his head and bolted across the bridge, the rest of the group following.

They moved quickly into the building, the single room smelling ancient, a thick layer of black dust covering the ground.

"Destruction approaches, yes, yes," Empech said. "We must be quick."

Gameknight surveyed the room. The walls were lined with bookshelves, the multicolored tomes dusty as if they hadn't been touched for years. Against one wall was a sloped table with three pieces of paper, complicated runes drawn on each. On the ground beneath the papers sat a book, opened to the first page.

"Look, another book," Weaver pointed out.

Gameknight bent down and picked up the book, then opened it to the first page. He found a large rectangle on the right page, the image dark and foreboding.

"He went into this Age," the User-that-is-not-a-user said.

"What?" Woodcutter asked.

"I told you all before, this mod, Mystcraft, lets you use these books as gateways to new dimensions within Minecraft," Gameknight explained. "This book leads to a new world . . . to a new Age."

A huge explosion of rock and dirt filled the air. A distant mountain disintegrated and disappeared from sight.

"Entity303, he went into this book," Gameknight repeated. "We must follow him. When we . . ."

There was a loud crash outside. Through the doorway, they could all see the ground around the library shake as if terrified of its own mortality, then fall away, leaving only small, isolated islands of black grass floating in the distance.

"Hurry!" Digger exclaimed.

"Herder, get the wolves close to me," Gameknight said. "Everyone else, grab on and hold tight."

"Do we need to make one of those linking books you made back in the dungeons of the White Castle?" Crafter asked.

"I don't think we'll be wanting to return here anytime soon," the User-that-is-not-a-user replied. "If there even still is a *here.* Everyone ready?"

"Here we go again," Stitcher said. "Time for another ride on the trans-dimensional minecart."

"I like that name," Gameknight said.

Stitcher smiled at her cleverness.

"Here we go."

The User-that-is-not-a-user placed his hand on the book, waited for a second to make sure everyone was touching him, then imagined himself clicking on it with his mouse. The purple-and-silver mist swirled about him like a thick morning fog, then they disappeared from the doomed library and traveled through the book to the next Age.

Soaring high overhead, a red demon watched the party in the abandoned library. His leathery black wings stretched out and carried him on the gentle breeze as he banked and curved. Suddenly, he felt the strangers disappear from this world.

"I havvve not felllt such magical enchannntments for a lonnng timmme," the creature said to the slowly disappearing world, his long, drawn-out words connected together, almost as if he were singing. "They havvve swords and armorrr with enchantments . . . potionnnns by the scores. I thirrrst for their maaagic."

The red monster, named Kahn, dove toward the library, then pulled up just before he slammed into the ground. Landing gracefully on his clawed red feet, Kahn folded in his dark, bat-like wings and entered the library. He had to stoop just a little to keep the straight, white horns on his head from scraping the top of the doorway.

A book lay on the ground. The demon looked at it and smiled, his white, razor-sharp teeth gleaming in the pale light of the diseased green sunlight that streamed in through a window.

"I would lllove to devourrr you, book," the monster said to the dusty tome, "but I mmmust follow the stranngers. Their enchannntments will feed me annnd make mmme stronnnger."

Reaching down, the demon touched the book with the tip of a clawed finger, then closed his eyes and followed his newfound prey into the next Age, just as the floor beneath him began to fall away into the void. The bright red demon disappeared in a cloud of purple and silver as the last remnants of the world crumbled to dust, leaving the dying Age forever empty.

CHAPTER 2
ENTITY303'S RAGE

Entity303 ran through the decrepit land with a smile on his face. Everything in this terrain bespoke death: the grass was an ashen gray, the sky was a dirty brown, the blood-red sun hung low in the sky, the rivers that zigzagged across the ground were an oily black, and the trees looked as if they were made from the skeleton of some kind of extinct prehistoric beast. Every tree was devoid of leaves, the central trunk a bleached white column of bone, with square joints positioned up the barren tree, narrower pieces of bone sticking out like skeletal arms, each ending in a thin, parched, calcified protrusion. The forest of bone trees stretched out in all directions but did not cover the entire terrain. Many places had nothing but gaping holes where once the landscape existed, but in this unstable Age, as with the last, the ground was quickly deteriorating.

Drawing his glowing, infused sword, Entity303 slashed at one of the pale trees in frustration, toppling it to the ground.

"That idiotic villager, Weaver, should have never escaped from me," the vile user groaned. "Having him as a hostage gave me an advantage." He looked down at the pieces of bone that now lay at his feet, the tree just a stump sticking up out of the ground. "It's no matter. When I find the Age I'm seeking, I'll have all the allies I need, and then we'll see if Gameknight and all his pathetic friends can survive my plans."

Entity303 laughed an evil, maniacal laugh that filled the air. He loved the sound of his own voice.

Glancing up from the bone trees, the user stared at the black, twisting structures that clawed their way between the bony branches. The crystals were made of something darker than coal; some block he didn't recognize. The crystalline structures were jagged shapes that somehow seemed as if they were the embodiment of pain and suffering. Entity303 thought they appeared to be made of the same thing that flowed through the rivers, but the liquid was thick and gloopy, like oil, and the crystals were shiny and polished. The entire world conveyed agony and suffering and death . . . it was fabulous.

Throughout the land, tiny green hobgoblins moved amidst the pale white trees. Their dark, olive-colored skin stood out in stark contrast to the pale white structures and the gray, lifeless-looking grass. With jagged noses and wide pointy ears, they would have appeared terrifying if it were not for their diminutive size; hobgoblins were only as tall as a village child. They each wore light brown shorts and no shirts, their exposed barrel chests rippling with muscles.

The creatures spotted Entity303, but ignored the user, as if he were just another part of the terrain; hobgoblins were typically peaceful . . . unless threatened, when they tended to swarm down upon the threat with sharp nails and pointy teeth.

Entity303 drank a potion of Leaping and a potion of Swiftness, then approached a group of tiny green monsters with his blazing yellow sword drawn.

"Come here, little hobgoblins, I have something for you," the user said with a vicious smile.

The edge of his weapon glowed bright yellow, as if powered from within. Entity303 suddenly struck at the creatures, destroying the first two quickly, just to let them all know he was serious. Swinging his glowing blade in a wide arc, Entity303 sliced into a large group of monsters, not doing much damage, but causing their rage to seethe and overflow. The monsters hissed like boiling teakettles, then charged at him. Leaping backward, the user put some distance between himself and the monsters, then removed his white yeti chest plate and replaced it with his gray Elytra wings. More hissing came from behind; the creatures were approaching from all sides . . . good.

"Come, my little monsters. Try and catch me, if you dare."

Sprinting toward a group of green, toothy monsters, Entity303 leapt up into the air just before reaching them. The creatures reached out with their pointed claws, but the user was already much too high, the potion of leaping giving the user extra height. At the apex, he leaned forward and allowed his wings to snap open. The Elytra wings caught the breeze and lifted him into the air, allowing him to soar over the oily rivers and dull gray landscape. The monsters stared up at him with furious red eyes. Reaching into his inventory, he pulled out splash potions of Poison and dropped them on the tiny hobgoblins, just because he could. Entity303 laughed cruelly as the poisoned creatures writhed on the ground in misery.

From this altitude, the bone trees that covered the land looked more like the spines of animals that had been trying to crawl up out of the ground, but became stuck and finally perished, with their skeletal remains now all that was left. He knew that wasn't the case, but the thought amused him.

Banking in a wide arc, Entity303 settled atop one of the inky-black crystalline structures. The tip of the jagged shape was high off the ground, far away from the hobgoblins' claws. Waiting for more to gather, Entity303 threw another splash potion on the creatures, this time one of Blindness, then jumped high into the air and glided away across the landscape.

A bolt of lightning suddenly stabbed at the ground from the dusty brown sky, the crooked white fingers of electricity slashing at the landscape and making chunks of land crumble into dust. Large sections of the biome just fell away, leaving gigantic holes through which the utter darkness of the void could be seen. Entity303 eyed the sky nervously as he flew, hoping he would not be the next target.

"I hope Gameknight999 and his friends enjoy following me," Entity303 said with a chuckle as he landed on the bleached limb of a bone tree.

Running across the pale branch, he leapt into the air just as a bolt of lightning struck the ground nearby, causing another rift to form in the ground, the landscape dissolving away.

Pulling out his bow, he fired at the hobgoblins below as he flew, not seeking to destroy, only to wound and enrage; it was working. The *Punch II* enchantment on the bow gave him a little speed boost that he didn't really need; these foolish creatures would never catch him even if he weren't flying. The green monsters glared up at him, growling and snarling with anger and frustration, all of them scurrying about, looking for a way to reach him as he soared overhead. Banking to the left, he spotted what he was looking for: a square, unadorned cobblestone building.

"The library!" he exclaimed.

Every Age had a library, and within each library was a trio of rune-covered pages.

"If that pathetic Gameknight999 hadn't rushed me, I'd have had all the pages I needed to get to King Iago's world," Entity303 growled, frustrated. "Now, he has the all-important page, and I must travel from Age to Age until I come across that page in one of the libraries."

In a fit of anger, he fired an arrow down at one of the hobgoblins. It struck the tiny monster in the shoulder, causing it to screech in pain. Entity303 smiled.

More lightning stabbed downward from the sky, some of the bolts landing amidst the hobgoblins, causing the puny creatures to plummet into the void, along with the land on which they stood. Entity303 laughed as the hobgoblins fell, screaming.

Leaning forward, Entity303 traded altitude for speed and streaked toward the abandoned structure. A few hobgoblins stood nearby, but he eliminated them with arrows before he landed; he did not want to be disturbed within the ancient structure. Landing with practiced ease, the evil user removed his wings and quickly replaced them with his white and blue Alpha-Yeti armor.

He looked up at the cobblestone structure. Stairs led up to the entrance of the library, where tall columns of stone on either side of the doorway reached up to the roof high overhead. With the colored spirals from the potions still circling about in his vision, Entity303 leaped quickly past the stairs and into the building. Instantly, his senses were assaulted by the age of the place. A musty smell permeated the interior, and a thick layer of dust covered everything, adding to the unpleasant aroma. The walls were lined with bookshelves, each brightly colored book marked on its spine with writing that had nearly faded. On one wall was a slanted writing table; he knew it to be a lectern, as it was called in this mod, Mystcraft. On it were three square pieces of parchment, with complex, curvilinear runes drawn on each.

He glanced at each paper quickly, then growled in frustration.

"The page I need isn't here!" Entity303 complained to the empty room. "Now, I must go to another random world, and another and another until I find the page I need. And all because of that annoying Gameknight999!"

The user took a set of rune-covered pages out of his inventory and laid them out on the ground. He had the Sky Islands, the Tall Forest, and all the other pages he needed; about thirty-seven pages in total, he knew.

There was just one missing: the Cave World sheet. With that page, his book would be complete, and Entity303 could use it to get to the world where his allies and supplies waited. But if any detail in the sequence of pages were wrong, or if a page were missing, then the incomplete book would take him to some random Age.

"If only I'd had to time to grab everything from that chest under the White Castle," he said, shaking his head.

He growled in frustration as the image of Gameknight999 and his friends charging at him in the dungeon under the White Castle filled his mind. If he'd had just a few seconds more, then he'd be executing the next phase of his plan right now, instead of wandering around looking for the right page, but that pesky User-that-is-not-a-user had gotten in the way. Eventually, Entity303 would find the Cave World page, and then his plans would resume, but he was impatient; he wanted to get the destruction of Minecraft started . . . now!

Thunder boomed outside as flashes of lightning lit the interior of the library . . . this unstable Age was not going to last long, Entity303 knew.

Ignoring the three pages on the lectern, Entity303 collected the pages off the ground and stuffed them into his inventory. He then removed his bookbinder from his inventory and placed it on the ground. Gathering a group of random pages he didn't need, he built another book. It didn't matter what the next world looked like; all that mattered was the library and the three pages contained within.

Pulling the newly constructed book from the bookbinder, he placed the device back into his inventory, then held the book in one hand.

Suddenly, the ground shook, causing the land directly around the library to fall into the void. Entity303 moved to the doorway and peered out. He saw that much of the terrain around the library was now gone, leaving a gap between the library and the land around it.

"I'm not done toying with you yet, Gameknight999. I want you to follow me, so that you can see the destruction of Minecraft firsthand," Entity303 said.

Using blocks of stone, he built a bridge from the library to the solid land around it, just as he had in the last world, making it possible for his pursuers to continue their hopeless chase. Sprinting across the bridge, he sped across the dull gray landscape, yelling at the top of his lungs. The hobgoblins heard his voice and came toward him from all directions, their hissing growing louder and louder.

"Yes, come get me, you pathetic monsters!" yelled the evil user.

He ran in a circle, leaping high into the air, making sure the monsters saw him, then ran back to the library.

"Come get me, you fools!" Entity303 yelled at them as they rushed toward him. "But beware, my army is following me and will be here soon. You had best prepare."

The hobgoblins began to congregate at the end of his little bridge, then ran across, the sharp claws on their tiny feet making a clicking sound on the cobblestone.

Entity303 glanced at the open door to the library and saw the creatures forming up, getting ready to charge. He laughed. The green monsters moved up the stairs and burst into the room, their red eyes glowing with rage. When they stepped into the strange library, they skidded to a stop and stared at the trapped user, each of them hissing and growling.

"My friends will be here soon; please welcome them," Entity303 said with a laugh, then touched the dark rectangle on the open book. Instantly, he was enveloped in a cloud of purple-and-silver smoke that made the hobgoblins step back, confused. Their demonic green faces then changed from expressions of rage to frustration as Entity303 slowly faded from sight. Watching their disappointment was priceless to Entity303 and made the terrible user laugh a malicious laugh that made the monsters cringe.

When he finally disappeared completely, and the echoes of his terrible laugh faded, the book landed on the ground with a thud. The hobgoblins growled and moved out of the library to spread across the landscape, waiting for those who followed, their razor-sharp claws gleaming in the light of the blood-red sun.

CHAPTER 3

TRAIL OF DESTRUCTION

The companions materialized in a cloud of purple-and-silver smoke. As always, a square of cobblestone that was five blocks by five blocks in size sat under their feet. It butted up against a field of gray grass, the ashen blades waving in the constant breeze that always flowed east-to-west.

Around them stood the strangest trees Gameknight had ever seen. They were bleached white with no leaves at all, the branches and trunks completely bare. Knobby joints connected the branches to the trunks, forming what looked like a boney knuckle. The branches stretched out from the tree not just at the top, like on an oak or junglewood tree, but all along its height, almost forming what looked like ribs in a skeleton, though they stuck out on all sides. The pale limbs reminded Gameknight999 of rungs on a ladder, every branch evenly spaced from those above and below.

"Bone trees," Empech said in a quiet and sad voice.

"I don't think I've ever seen something as sad as these trees," Stitcher said in a quiet voice. "They look like the physical representation of death."

"The trees are not the only sad things, yes, yes," the tiny gray-skinned gnome said. He moved across the dull grass and stepped up to a stream that gurgled nearby. "Look at the water in this wounded land. It flows as black as a shadow at midnight."

The group walked to the narrow brook and looked down. The dark liquid flowed slowly past, moving like thick honey, occasional bubbles of noxious gas rising to the surface. Gameknight reached down to touch it, but Empech's three-fingered hand suddenly settled upon his outstretched arm and stopped him.

"It is likely poison, yes, yes," the pech said. "Best not to touch."

"Only Gameknight999 would reach out and touch a river of black goo," Hunter said with a smile.

Gameknight gave her a mocking frown, then smiled.

One of the wolves howled, its voice filled with pride and strength.

"Something's coming," Herder said.

"Everyone, put away your weapons," Gameknight said. "Herder, bring the wolves in close; we don't want to frighten those who approach."

Herder put his stubby rectangular fingers to the corners of his mouth and whistled. The high-pitched sound was piercing and cut through the air like a knife. Instantly, the wolves came running, gathering around the lanky boy. He knelt and patted the animals on their sides, his long, stringy black hair swaying back and forth.

Suddenly, a pair of creatures ran across a gray, grass-covered hill nearby, their pointed ears and bright red eyes giving them an almost demonic look, but the deep, forest-green color of their skin was a welcome contrast to the black water, dirty brown sky, skeletal trees, and strange dark crystalline structures that stretched up out of the ground. Another small group of creatures could be seen following the first.

"Hobgoblins," Empech said, a smile on his oversized head.

"Are they dangerous?" Digger asked.

"Only if provoked," the tiny gnome replied.

The two hobgoblins approached the party as the small cluster that followed was just cresting the hill. A hissing sound could be heard from the approaching monsters.

"That doesn't seem like a good sound," Hunter said with concern.

"They are angry, yes, yes," Empech said, surprised.

Everyone tensed. Hunter and Stitcher pulled out their bows and notched arrows to their strings. The wolves growled as their fur bristled, their tails sticking straight out. Gameknight stepped forward and walked slowly and calmly toward the two creatures, his arms outstretched to show that he wasn't armed. His diamond armor seemed to glow in the strange light of the blood-red sun. As the monsters closed, they drew back their lips, showing row upon row of pointed teeth.

"We don't want to fight you," Gameknight said calmly. "We're just visitors here, following someone who passed through your land."

"Your commander told us you would arrive," the taller of the two hobgoblins growled. "You will not be allowed to take over our land."

"We don't want your land," Gameknight began to say, but the hobgoblins ignored him and attacked.

The shorter of the two leapt forward and slashed, its sharp claws scratching across the User-that-is-not-a-user's diamond chest plate. The taller monster then dove toward Gameknight, trying to wrap its stubby arms around his head. The user rolled to the side, then stood with his iron and diamond swords drawn.

"Please . . . we don't want to fight!" Gameknight pleaded.

The monsters charged, trying to bite and scratch at his flesh. Their razor-sharp claws and teeth screeched as they slid across his diamond armor. Suddenly, a wave of white fur appeared in front of Gameknight999. The wolves drove the creatures back with small nips to their arms and legs, but when they would not relent, the battle became serious. The two creatures slashed at the wolves with their claws, tearing out tufts of fur.

"Wolves . . . attack!" Herder commanded, no sympathy for the little hobgoblins in his voice.

Just then, the trailing group of monsters approached, their hissing making it sound as if they each held a poisonous viper. The wolves formed a wall of fur and fangs, pressing their bodies close together to deny any monster the chance to slip past. Instantly, the hobgoblins dove at the wolves, tearing handfuls of white fur from the animals' lean bodies. The wolves yelped in pain, then turned vicious and attacked. Hunter and Stitcher added their arrows to the attack, hoping to only wound the little creatures, but the green monsters would not relent. The fired as fast as they could, but there were too many hobgoblins for the wolves and archers to hold them back.

"We're too exposed here," Woodcutter said as he stepped forward, his shining axe flashing through the air like metallic lightning. "We need to find some place that's defendable until we can figure out what to do."

"What about that place over there?" Herder asked. The lanky boy had climbed up into the bone trees and was pointing off to the west.

"What do you see?" Gameknight asked. He slashed at a hobgoblin that had managed to get past the wolves. The monster's claws left another set of scratches across his diamond armor, cutting deep grooves into the crystalline coating. His iron sword clashed with the sharp nails, then his diamond sword landed a solid hit, causing the creature to flash red with damage. Gameknight kicked the monster hard in the chest, sending it flying backward. It stood for a moment and eyed the two swords, then let out a loud screech and ran away.

"It seems to be a building like from the last world, with tall columns standing before a wide door," Herder said, his long black hair falling across his face as he climbed to the top of the bone tree.

"That's it, the library," Gameknight said. "We need to go there."

A huge group of hobgoblins flowed across the distant hill like an angry green tide, their claws shining bright in the light of the red sun high overhead. Dark brown clouds slowly moved in from the east. Something about those clouds seemed wrong to Gameknight, as if they were somehow a threat.

"We'll never be able to cross the land with that bigger army approaching," Digger said, his voice cracking with fear.

The stocky NPC was holding Tux, Gameknight's pet penguin, under one arm. Next to him stood Empech, the magical gnome's crystalline blue eyes darting about nervously. A group of green monsters charged at Weaver, but Woodcutter was there to push them back, his shining axe cleaving through the attackers as Weaver's iron sword danced past sharp claws to find soft green flesh. The monsters flashed red and fell, disappearing with *a pop*.

"Climb up here into the bone trees," Herder yelled.

"That's a great idea, Herder," Gameknight said. "Everyone into the trees. We'll go from bone tree to bone tree until we reach the library. The hobgoblins are too short to get up here. Good thinking, Herder."

Gameknight climbed up into the pale white bone limbs, then turned and reached down to help the person behind him. Below, he saw Weaver glaring at Herder, a look of rabid jealousy on his square face.

"Weaver, come on, give me your hand."

The young boy glanced at Gameknight999, then moved to the next tree and climbed up just as a group of hobgoblins closed in on him. He scurried into the bare treetops, barely avoiding the sharp claws and pointed teeth.

"Herder, have your wolves go to the library and secure it for us," Gameknight said.

"No problem," the boy said.

Herder gave two short whistles, then pointed to the abandoned library. The wolves seemed to know exactly what he meant and sprinted off toward the cobblestone building, their white fur visible as they weaved between the bright green bodies of the hobgoblins. Some of the monsters tried to strike at the animals, but the wolves' loping gait was so fast, the tiny creatures couldn't lay a single claw on them.

"Nice," Gameknight said softly.

Herder smiled with pride.

Weaver scowled at Herder, trying to hide his jealousy from Gameknight but doing a poor job.

"The world falls apart. We must hurry, yes, yes," Empech said.

They ran along the narrow, bone-white branches, leaping from one tree to the next. The skeletal limbs gave their jumps a little springy boost, allowing them to easily reach the next tree. As they moved across the barren forest, Gameknight noticed the hobgoblins were now wandering about in all directions, only a small number staying directly underneath the party.

"Everyone stop for a minute and be quiet," Gameknight whispered.

They all stood motionless atop the forest of bones. The lack of sound seemed to confuse the hobgoblins, and those beneath moved off in search of their enemy.

"I don't think they have very good eyesight," Herder said in a low voice.

"I think Herder is correct," Gameknight whispered.

"Of course you do," Weaver said under his breath.

Weaver glared at Herder, the young boy's bright blue eyes filled with jealousy at Gameknight's praise. He still hadn't forgiven Gameknight for lying to him in the past about posing as the great Smithy of the Two-swords. Weaver had trusted Gameknight and felt betrayed for the deception, having made his feelings known just after his rescue from the clutches of Entity303.

The User-that-is-not-a-user saw the worrisome look aimed at Herder and sighed.

There's too much anger and distrust in Weaver, Gameknight thought. *I must do something to get him to forgive me.*

But he didn't know what. Weaver was filled with such anger that it worried him. And the young boy suspected Gameknight was keeping more information from him. Weaver was critical to Minecraft's history, teaching many, including Crafter, how to use TNT in battle. But the User-that-is-not-a-user couldn't tell the boy why he was so important; that knowledge might change how he'd act. If Gameknight told Weaver too much, he might change history and damage Minecraft, just like Entity303 had.

"Here's what we're gonna do," Gameknight said softly. "I'll drink a potion of Swiftness, then run off and draw the hobgoblins away. I want all of you to get to the library and set up some defenses. I can't imagine this world was what Entity303 was running to, but I'm sure he went to the library like in the last Age."

"This plan seems unusually risky to me," Crafter said with concern.

"That seems kinda normal to me," Hunter said, "as it *is* one of Gameknight's plans."

"Look, we need to get those hobgoblins to move away from the library so all of you can get to it," Gameknight explained. "If someone else wants to be the bait, then speak up."

"Oh, suddenly, this seems like a great plan," Hunter said.

Stitcher punched her in the arm.

"What'd I say?" the older sister complained.

Stitcher just rolled her eyes.

"This is the way it's gonna be," Gameknight said, his tone telling all of them the discussion was over. "All of you ready?"

His friends nodded their blocky heads.

Before Gameknight could reach into his inventory, Empech had already pulled a glass bottle from his pack, a light blue liquid sloshing about within. The tiny, gray-skinned gnome leapt to the adjacent bone-tree limb and handed him the bottle, his large, oversized face gazing up at the User-that-is-not-a-user with a smile. Gameknight took the bottle and drank the liquid. Instantly, colorful spirals appeared around his head.

"As soon as the monsters are gone, move to the library."

Sprinting with enhanced speed, Gameknight zipped to the end of the bone-branch, then jumped off. He landed on the ground without slowing. As he ran, the User-that-is-not-a-user drew his swords and banged them together, making a *CLANGING* sound.

"COME ON, FOLLOW ME, HOBGOBLINS!" Gameknight shouted.

The monsters turned toward the sound and ran like mice after a piece of cheese. In minutes, a green wave of claws and pointed teeth had passed out of the bone-tree forest and into a clearing of gray grass and small black bushes. Gameknight sprinted in a wide circle, drawing all the creatures to him while he watched his friends quickly scurry to the library. Zigzagging across the field, he led the monsters on a circuitous chase while the others built stone walls near the cobblestone building's entrance. When they were completed, Gameknight put away his swords and bolted for the structure.

When he approached the building, two heads with bright red hair appeared above the top of the hastily constructed wall, enchanted bows in their hands.

"Can you run any slower?!" Hunter shouted down at him.

"The swiftness potion just wore off," Gameknight replied.

"Well, you better hurry, or you're gonna become a hobgoblin snack," the redhead replied with alarm.

Behind him, the User-that-is-not-a-user could hear the hissing of the monsters hot on his heels. A pair of flaming arrows streaked past him. They were followed by two high-pitched screams that came from disturbingly close behind him. Gameknight poured on the speed and ran across the narrow bridge that led to the library, dashing through an opening in the barricade. Digger quickly filled the hole with blocks of dirt.

Squawk! Tux said, the little penguin obviously glad to have Gameknight back.

"I'm glad you thought to put the bridge there," Gameknight said to Crafter.

"It was already there," the young NPC replied.

Suddenly, the sky boomed as lightning flashed across the sky and hit the ground. Gameknight saw the land begin to crumble and fall away under the stabbing blades of glowing electricity.

"This world will not last long," Empech said. "Haste would be good."

Gameknight nodded, then stepped into the library. As with all abandoned libraries in Mystcraft, this one had walls lined with bookshelves, the dusty tomes in every color and size. On the slanted desk were three pieces of paper, like in the last one, each untouched. A book lay on the ground with its pages open. The wolf pack leader sniffed the book, then growled.

"He was here," Herder snarled. "The wolves can sense it . . . and so can I."

"I think you're becoming part wolf now, Wolf-man," Hunter said with a smile.

Herder glanced at the girl and scowled.

"I don't joke about my wolves," he snarled and moved to the corner.

"Wow, he's serious about those dogs," Weaver said quietly.

"Shhh," Woodcutter said. "Don't ever call them dogs. Herder will get really angry, and then the wolves will get really angry, and then who knows what will happen."

"They're just dogs," Weaver said under his breath.

The ground shook as shafts of lightning stabbed down at the surface of Minecraft, thunder echoing across the land. The ground shuddered as if in pain.

"Why do you think Entity303 led us straight back to another library?" Crafter asked. "This is the same thing as the last world."

"I think he must be looking for something," Gameknight said. "Remember, Weaver said Entity303 had mentioned losing something in one of the Ages."

"Yeah," Weaver chimed in. "He told me that while I was his prisoner in the Twilight Forest."

"I think he's looking for that thing, but he doesn't know where it is," Gameknight said.

"So he's randomly going from world to world to find it?" Hunter asked. "Wouldn't that take, like, forever?"

"Maybe," Gameknight replied. "But we have no choice. We must follow him until we can catch him."

"Well, we can't just stand around here chatting about it," Digger said as he bent down and picked up Tux, then turned to Gameknight999. "We need to get out of here, fast. Do your book thing."

Another lightning strike hit the ground nearby, causing the land to shake as if mortally wounded. Dust fell from the shelves, creating a gray haze in the air. Gameknight coughed.

"Let's get going," Hunter said. "Come on, quick."

The User-that-is-not-a-user nodded, then waited for everyone to move where they could touch him. The wolves moved in tight, then Gameknight touched the book and the party disappeared from the land of the hobgoblins. None of them noticed the huge, red creature floating in lazy circles high in the air, its dark bat-wings riding gracefully on the breeze, its eyes fixed on the library and its occupants.

CHAPTER 4

KAHN

The huge demon had appeared on the cobblestone pad after the villagers had moved toward the black, poisonous river. Instantly, he took to the sky, flapping his thick, leathery wings and hiding in a small cloud overhead. He watched with curiosity as the party of villagers ran across the landscape, running from the pathetically weak hobgoblins. They could have easily defeated the little green monsters with their weapons, but instead, they ran?

"Why dooo you runnn from thooose monsterssss?" Kahn said, his words drawn out into long, deep tones.

Flapping his wide, black wings to gain more altitude, he floated high above the clouds. Gliding on the warm, gusty currents, Kahn found a spot where he could see the villagers from between two large clouds. He was shocked to find the NPCs foolishly retreating across the land. Rather than fight, it seemed the strangers chose to run across the tops of the bone trees. The magical demon, Kahn, found this strange. It was as if they didn't want to destroy the ridiculous hobgoblins for some reason.

He banked to the right, then drew in his shadowy wings and descended, trading altitude for speed. He shot through a thick cloud, hoping to get closer to the villagers. Sparkling electricity danced throughout the misty rectangle, the charges slithering across his thick, leathery skin like tiny, energized spiders. It made his flesh tingle, the few hairs on the back of his neck standing straight up. Kahn could feel the charge building . . . soon, the lightning would strike.

He flapped his wings to pick up speed, then shot from one cloud to the next, slowly closing in on the newcomers. Suddenly Kahn sensed magic, strong magic. It was as if a beacon had just been lit, the magical source shining bright on the mundane landscape of this pathetic world. A hunger blossomed from deep within his soul, then radiated outward to the tips of his bat-like wings. Magic; strong, wonderful magic. He craved it . . . had to have it. Magic was what fed Kahn, and consuming the enchanted powers caused the mighty demon to grow stronger and more lethal.

"I havvve not devourrred magic this stronnng in yearrrrs," Kahn said in a deep, rumbling voice.

The scent of the supernatural energy was intoxicating, making his toothy mouth water, his two white tusks gleaming with moisture.

Quickly, the red monster dove to the ground and hid behind a cluster of bone trees. A group of hobgoblins saw him land and charged, a hissing coming from behind their pointed white teeth. Kahn smiled, then flicked his clawed hand toward them with disdain. A small ball of fire came to life and streaked to the pathetic creatures, the deadly sphere wreathed in lethal purple flames. It struck the group and exploded, destroying the hobgoblins, their cries of fear and despair comically filling the air.

The demon turned back toward the villagers, but they had already ducked into the library, the last one passing through the puny cobblestone wall they'd erected across the opening. And then, Kahn felt them disappear from this world and move to another dimension.

"That maaagic felt sooo fammmiliar," Kahn mused to himself as he licked his thin, dark lips.

He walked through the bone-tree forest, moving closer to the abandoned library. Bolts of lightning stabbed at the ground, causing patches of the land to just dissolve away and fall into the void. Thunder boomed overhead, its volume so overwhelming that Kahn thought the sky itself might be splitting open.

The hobgoblins looked nervously upward, but when they saw Kahn, their pent up rage burst forth and they charged, their growling, hissing voices adding to the cacophony.

He turned and glared at them, then flicked his hand again. Balls of fire streaked from his dark-red palm and smashed into the monsters, instantly engulfing them in flames, the blast of the attack throwing them backward a dozen blocks. More of the pathetic green creatures charged at him, unaware of the futility of their attack. Kahn threw more balls of fire, then charged.

With dark claws extended from each finger, the red demon fell upon the foolish hobgoblins, intent on teaching them a lesson about when to attack and when to run for their lives. He slashed at them, his razor-sharp claws tearing through their HP with single swipes. Ducking his head, he barreled into them, the two long, white horns protruding from his head as deadly as any sword. Flicking his wings open, Kahn spun in a circle, the hooked claws at the end of each wing smashing into the monsters, causing them to flash red with damage. The demon destroyed hobgoblins by the scores, spinning across the battlefield like a whirlwind of clawed destruction. He tore through their numbers as if they were insignificant pieces of paper.

Finally, the last few survivors realized their folly and retreated, leaving Kahn alone. He thought about throwing balls of purple fire at the retreating monsters, but instead discarded the idea and focused on his real prey.

More lightning tore into the landscape, causing the land under the fleeing hobgoblins to fall away, dropping the last few survivors into the void.

"This worrrld is also dying," Kahn growled. "Jussst like the lassst."

Something was happening to Minecraft . . . something bad.

He turned back toward the library. Lightning struck the ground near him, causing the gray grass to shudder, then fall apart and plummet into the darkness. Kahn flapped his great wings and soared into the library. Like before, he found an open book on the ground, the dusty tome radiating with supernatural powers. Reaching out with a single, pointed black claw, he touched the dark rectangle on the page, then used his own enchantments to dive through the gateway, the scent of his magical prey burning bright.

"I willll havvve you soon," Kahn said, his long, deep voice echoing in the room as a cloud of purple-and-silver mist enveloped him.

And then he was gone.

CHAPTER 5

TROUBLE WITH TRUTH

Gameknight stepped off the cobblestone platform into a new Age. He found himself in a field of knee-high grass that waved back and forth under the gentle caress of the constant east-to-west breeze. Overhead was a cloudless sky that stretched from horizon to horizon, the sun hanging high in the air.

A few trees dotted the landscape, with small bushes adorning the hills and plains. It all seemed peaceful and idyllic except for the fact that everything was devoid of color. The grass was a dark gray, and the sky was ashen as well. The leaves on the trees were light gray, almost silver, with the trunks a mixture of charcoals and grays and black. The only things that offered a break in the monotony of gray tones were Gameknight and his friends. It was as if they'd stepped into a black-and-white movie somehow, but they themselves were still in color.

"What's going on here?" Stitcher asked. "This doesn't seem natural."

"The land is wounded, yes, yes," Empech said. "Much is out of balance here."

Gameknight glanced at the pech and could see worry in his crystalline blue eyes. The gnome's lower jaw stuck out just a little from the top, as usual, but with the tight-lipped grimace on the creature's face; he looked enraged. Moving to his side, the User-that-is-not-a-user gently placed a hand on the gnome's small shoulders. He felt Empech slowly relax, the muscles in the tiny body finally unclenching.

"Where are all the animals?" Herder asked.

"Or villagers," Weaver said, eyeing Herder with an accusatory glance; his glare saying *You care more for animals than people.*

"I've never seen an Age like this before," Gameknight said.

"How many different worlds are there within this mod?" Crafter asked.

"Well, an infinite number," Gameknight replied. "You remember those pages that are always in the library?"

Crafter nodded.

"Those pages are used to create the books that get you here," Gameknight explained. "If anything is missing in the book, like the Sky Color page, or the Biome page, then Mystcraft just adds something random. Usually, this ends up with an unstable Age like we've seen in the past two worlds."

"It doesn't seem like a very reliable system," Stitcher said, confused.

"I know, but it's how it was programmed by the developers," Gameknight replied. "This world here probably had something missing from the book Entity303 used, and this is what that evil user created."

"Your adversary did not create this world," Empech said. "Entity303 only formed the gateway to it, yes yes. It has existed for many lifetimes."

"But then why does it look so . . . strange?" Digger asked.

"The book Entity303 uses was probably just a arbitrary collection of pages," Gameknight said. "Apparently, he's just randomly going through these Ages and doesn't care if they're unstable. He's in search of . . . something."

"Not unstable always," Empech said, his high-pitched voice barely a whisper. "This world is strained like the last, yes, yes, Empech can feel it. Your enemy, Entity303, caused this with the mods he's added to Minecraft. The fabric between worlds slowly tears more and more."

Gameknight glanced around at the dull gray surroundings. At one time, this had likely been a beautiful meadow, with a bright blue sky and tall oak trees in the distance. But now, all the color had been drained from the land and replaced with shadows. A tiny square tear seeped from his eye and tumbled down his cheek.

"Woodcutter, doesn't a land with so few trees look sad to you?" Crafter asked.

"I don't know; my brother was the one who really liked trees," Woodcutter said. "Given the choice, I prefer the dark shadows of a cave."

Crafter looked at the tall NPC, a look of confusion in his bright blue eyes.

Woodcutter pulled out his axe and passed it deftly from one hand to the next, ready for anything. He was the tallest of the company, with a thick head of dark brown hair that matched his equally dark eyes . . . they always seemed so sad. His bright red smock was vibrant and almost shocking next to the gray upon gray of this land.

"Woodcutter, I've know you for a long time now, but I just realized you never talk about your brother," Crafter said.

"No, I don't," the tall villager replied, a finality to his voice that silenced any discussion.

Crafter looked at Gameknight, a look of surprise on his young face. The User-that-is-not-a-user just shrugged, but cast a worried glance at the tall woodsman.

"Come on, everyone, let's find the library in this world and get out of here," Hunter interjected. "This place gives me the creeps."

"Wolves . . . track," Herder commanded.

Instantly, the white animals spread out in all directions, cutting through the tall gray grass like sharks cruising through dark seas. Their fur stood out as blazingly bright, making them easy to spot. One of the animals off to the left barked suddenly once, then gave off a proud howl that echoed across the dull landscape.

"They found it," Herder exclaimed, pleased. "I knew they would."

"Good job, Herder," Gameknight praised.

Weaver gave the lanky boy a scowl, which the User-that-is-not-a-user saw out of the corner of his eye.

I must do something to ease the tension building up in Weaver, Gameknight thought.

"Everyone, spread out and move carefully," the User-that-is-not-a-user said, his voice ringing with a tone of command and confidence. "This land seems peaceful, but we should still be cautious. The last world didn't seem that bad at first either."

"At least not until the massive army of hobgoblins appeared," Hunter added with a smile.

"Exactly," the User-that-is-not-a-user continued. "So, everyone spread out. Weaver, how about you watch the right flank with me?"

The young boy looked up and glanced at Gameknight, his blue eyes filled with irritation. With a shrug, he walked to the right and followed the lead wolf.

"Weaver, you seem angry," Gameknight started to say. "I think we should . . ."

"Why did you lie to me back during the Great Zombie Invasion?" the young boy blurted out.

The others in the party tried to move away a little to give the pair some privacy.

"I thought you understood why," Gameknight explained as they walked. "When Smithy was killed, I had to take his place, or the entire army would have fallen apart. If the Great Zombie Invasion hadn't been a success, then Herobrine would have destroyed everything."

"You could have trusted me, at least, but no . . . you shut me out." The expression in Weaver's blue eyes changed from simmering irritation to resentment and anger. "I *could* have been trusted, but instead, you kept me out when I could have helped."

"It was too dangerous, Weaver. If anyone had found out, the whole army could have fallen apart. Only Fencer and myself knew."

"You told Fencer, though!" the boy protested.

"He was there when Smithy died, Weaver. Fencer saw Smithy hand me his blacksmith's hammer and helmet. Only the two of us knew the truth. I asked Fencer multiple times if I could tell everyone else, but he felt it would have destroyed the hope that the villagers so precariously held onto." He moved closer so their shoulders were touching. "If I had said anything to anyone, Herobrine could have won the war."

"So what are you hiding now?" Weaver accused. "I know all this about Entity303 and the mods in Minecraft are tied to me somehow, but you won't really tell me anything. Why is that? What happens with Herobrine in the future? Why can't you trust me and tell me the truth?!"

The boy glared up at Gameknight, anger pulsing through every muscle, the tension in him like a coiled spring, ready to burst.

Gameknight knew he couldn't tell the boy everything; the more Weaver knew about his future, the more damage it could do to the timeline when Weaver went back into the past. He had to keep as much from Weaver as possible so the timeline could progress normally, without any knowledge of the future altering decisions made in the past.

The dangers of time travel made his head ache.

"You see . . . you're keeping things from me right now! I can tell you're thinking about everything you aren't gonna tell me. What is it . . . you don't trust me?" Weaver yelled.

"You know that's not the case," Gameknight said. "It's just that . . . it's complicated."

"Yeah . . . right. Can you tell *him*?" Weaver said, pointing to Herder up at the front of the formation. The lanky boy was walking next to the wolf pack leader, patting the furry animal on the side. "All he cares about are his animals, but you trust him more than you trust me."

"That's not true," the User-that-is-not-a-user replied, but the confident tone in his voice was fading.

"Oh yeah? Then tell me why I'm so important!"

"Well, Entity303 took you from the past so he could add these mods to Minecraft," Gameknight explained, hoping that would be enough.

"What do I have to do with the mods?" Weaver asked.

"I'm not sure, maybe it was because of . . ." Gameknight stopped. He could think of a lot of reasons why Weaver was the key, but they all involved things that happened in the young boy's future. Revealing those things could alter the timeline and cause Weaver to react differently, which would change everything . . . he couldn't say any more.

"You see . . . you're keeping things from me again. You don't trust me." Weaver said in an accusatory voice. Gameknight could see the hurt and distrust in the boy's steely blue eyes. The youth was about to say something when a sound drifted to their ears, stopping his comment. It was an unexpected noise that seemed somehow out of place.

"Is that . . . chickens?" Stitcher asked.

"I think so," Crafter asked.

Just then, the wolves on the left flank barked, then separated, allowing a group of small white creatures to weave through the long blades of grass, their yellow beaks parting the dark vegetation like a ship's fog lights cutting through gray mist. A group of at least twenty chickens approached, their clucks and cheeps adding the first traces of sound to the landscape other than the wind. The presence of the peaceful, innocent creatures brought a smile to all their faces. Some of the wolves growled hungrily, but Herder kept the animals in control, keeping the feathery creatures safe.

"Awhh . . . look, there are some babies," Stitcher said as she knelt and held out a hand.

The baby chick scurried up to Stitcher and nibbled on an outstretched finger, making the young girl giggle. Hunter moved to her side and bent over, offering a finger to another of the little animals.

Tux squawked excitedly, causing Digger to put the animal on the ground. The little penguin approached the chickens, uncertain at first, but when they clucked and brushed against her, she relaxed. Approaching the babies, Tux squawked once, getting their attention. The little chicks then ran toward the penguin, chasing her through the grass. Gameknight laughed, as did the others, the little game they were watching lightening their hearts for the first time since they'd come into Mystcraft.

Suddenly, another clucking sound trickled in through the grass, but this one was different; it sounded strained and angry. The wolves to the right growled but were still held firmly in check by Herder's will . . . somehow. They parted, allowing something into the circle of fangs and fur.

All Gameknight could see pushing through the tall grass was something dark purple with bright lavender eyes. The creatures moved with a jerky kind of motion, like robots slightly damaged or creatures possessed . . . like zombies on TV.

"What are those things?" Gameknight asked.

No one answered; all of his companions were watching Tux and the chicks play together, smiles on all of their blocky faces . . . all except Weaver, who still stood nearby.

"They remind me of those Endermen Herobrine used against us," Weaver said as he slowly slid his iron sword from his inventory.

"They look diseased or something," Gameknight said.

"Tainted, yes, yes," Empech said as the shadowy fowl approached. "They are tainted with the disease that spreads through Minecraft."

"Are they dangerous?" Gameknight asked as the group of dark chickens approached.

Before the little gnome could respond, the purple creatures opened their black beaks, showing rows of needle-like, stained teeth, their pointed tips gleaming under the pale sun. The little monsters fell upon the nearest chickens, attacking with a vengeance. The feathery white creatures screeched in pain as the tainted monsters tore into their HP. Gameknight pulled out his bow and shot at the nearest abomination, the *Flame* enchantment on his bow causing the projectile to light with magical fire across the pointed tip. His arrow hit the tainted chicken, but the monster did not stop its attack. It continued to tear into its target, ignoring the damage being done to its own HP.

"Everyone, run!" Gameknight shouted.

Bending over, he scooped up Tux and ran. The penguin squawked in protest, but the User-that-is-not-a-user didn't listen. He put away his bow and drew his diamond sword, eyes scanning the dark grass for purple threats.

More of the tainted chickens approached. They spread like a diseased purple wave, unstoppable and unrelenting. Glancing over his shoulder, Gameknight saw some of the white chickens slowly turn a dark purple as the tainted creatures passed on their poison to their white cousins.

"Look at the ground over there." Woodcutter said, pointing off to the right with his axe. "The ground and grass are the same color purple as those chickens."

"That is the source of the taint, yes, yes," Empech said. "The land will begin to tear at that spot, then spread as the taint covers the land."

"Is there something we can do to make it stop?" Stitcher asked. She spotted an infected chicken approaching and shot an arrow at the monster, the magical fire at the end of the shaft causing the creature to burst into flames. "We must help this land!"

"There is no hope," the tiny gnome said. He reached up and adjusted the straps on his huge backpack, the contents jingling back and forth as he ran. "Stop Entity303, yes, yes, that is all that can be done."

One of the wolves gave off a loud howl, then took off in a sprint, others in the pack following.

"They found the scent again," Herder said with pride.

Weaver growled softly, then shouted. "I see the library!"

"Yeah, I see it too," Gameknight said. He turned to say something to Weaver, but the boy was already scowling; he didn't compliment him fast enough. "Good job, Weaver," he said, but Weaver was no longer listening.

They dashed across the landscape, seeing more spots of tainted grass and stone spreading across the world. When they reached the cobblestone structure, they saw the same thing as before; three pieces of parchment lay undisturbed on the lectern, and a book sat open on the ground.

"He still hasn't found what he's looking for," Crafter noted, pointing to the three undisturbed sheets of paper and the book.

"I think you're right," Gameknight replied. "Everyone, come close."

He handed Tux to Digger, then waited for everyone to gather, the wolves pressing their furry bodies against armored legs.

The screeching of the tainted chickens was getting louder. They sounded as if they were just outside of the library.

Reaching out to the book, the User-that-is-not-a-user concentrated, imagining he was moving his mouse over the dark rectangle on the open page, then right-clicking on it as he would have if he were actually playing the Mystcraft mod.

What will be in store for us next? Gameknight thought. Tiny needles of fear jabbed at his every nerve, and then the companions were gone, leaving only the strange purple taint slowly enveloping the world, and, high overhead, a bright red creature stealthily riding the winds on black wings, his eyes glowing bright with ravenous hunger.

CHAPTER 6

FROZEN LAND

The cobblestone platform in the next Age was surrounded by columns of ice that stretched high into the air, like the ice spikes of the Overworld. But these frozen structures were much taller than anything any of the companions had ever seen, the glacial blue pillars stretching up thirty blocks if not more. To Gameknight999, they looked like massive spears of ice sticking up from the ground, as if some mythical giant had thrust them up through the snowy ground from some deep subterranean chamber. The bright sun overhead sent rays through the crystalline structures, breaking the light up into rainbow colors that splashed down onto the snowy landscape. Red and greens and blues and yellows stretched across the ground, coloring the snow like sheets of multi-flavored cotton candy. Gameknight imagined this was how it looked if you stood inside a kaleidoscope . . . it was fantastic.

"What is this place?" Digger asked in wonder as he set Tux on the ground.

Instantly, the little penguin flopped down on her side and rolled around on the ground, the cold, frozen carpet caressing her skin. She squawked and squeaked with delight. Stitcher smiled and sat down next to the penguin, picked up balls of snow and rubbed them against her black and white body, Tux purring contentedly.

Gameknight moved to a small hill and climbed to the top. Carefully, he surveyed the landscape, looking for any of the purple taint that had infected the last world. The land was completely covered with snow and ice, the white terrain only broken by the occasional dark trunks of trees, the normally green-shaded leaves frozen to a glacial blue. Strange jagged shafts of translucent ice stuck up into the air, twisting and arching in every way possible, forming complex crystalline structures. It was as if the giant forms had been moving, dancing in every way possible, then had been suddenly frozen, their dance violently stilled. Though Gameknight found the shapes beautiful, they were also disturbing, and made the back of his neck prickle with warning.

"Pretty incredible landscape." Crafter moved to his side and looked out across the biome. "It's like the ice spikes biomes of the Overworld, but even more fantastic."

"Sure, if you like freezing," Hunter added as she crunched her way to the top of the hill.

Gameknight glanced at each of them and smiled. "It's fantastic the way the sunlight goes through those icy pillars and the . . ."

"Village," Hunter snapped suddenly.

"The what?" the User-that-is-not-a-user asked, confused.

"I said 'Village'," the girl replied, her curly red hair looking unusually bright against the frozen landscape. "There's a village over there." She pointed with her enchanted bow.

Gameknight turned and peered in the direction she pointed. In the distance, a village was visible, the houses made of snow and packed ice blending in with the background. A tower made of light blue ice loomed high over the village, the top covered with snow. It reminded Gameknight of a frosted blueberry popsicle. He smiled.

"This land is in pain, like the last, yes, yes," Empech said in his high-pitched voice.

Gameknight turned and looked down at the little gnome. The pech shook, but not from cold. The User-that-is-not-a-user could see the look of fear in his deep blue, gem-like eyes. Something wasn't right.

"What's happening here?" Gameknight asked.

"It is not clear, but something is wrong, yes, yes." Empech replied, his voice shaking.

"We should check the village," Crafter said. "Make sure everyone there is okay."

"Maybe you're right," Gameknight replied.

One of the wolves barked, then gave off a loud howl.

"My wolves found Entity303's scent," Herder said. "He went that way." The boy pointed in the direction opposite from the village, toward two wide mountains. "We should follow."

"I think we need to check the village first," Gameknight said.

"But the trail . . ." Herder said.

"Sometimes people are more important than animals," Weaver interrupted, his voice ringing with anger.

A wolf next to Herder growled, his fur bristling.

"It's fine, Weaver," Gameknight said. "Herder just wants to keep the wolves on a fresh scent."

Herder nodded, his long, tangled hair falling across his face.

Weaver just smirked.

"I'm going to the village to check it out," the User-that-is-not-a-user continued. "All of you can stay here if you want."

Squawk, squawk! Tux said, then scurried up the hill and stood at Gameknight's side.

"I have to agree with Tux," Hunter said. "Let's follow Gameknight999."

"Everyone get bows out and keep your eyes open," the User-that-is-not-a-user ordered. "We need to be ready just in case Entity303 left some kind of surprise here for us."

They moved out, following Gameknight999 as he ran toward the village. His breath created a billowing cloud of mist, his nose and lips growing cold and getting slightly numb. His fingers ached as he squeezed his bow, but he didn't want to put it away; that itch at the back of his neck still warned him something was amiss.

A growl sounded off to the left. It was a polar bear with two of her cubs. The huge animal stood up on its back feet and snarled at the party, its eyes and nose dark as charcoal. The creature extended black claws from the end of its front paws and waved them in the air. Instantly, Gameknight veered to the right, wanting to keep as much distance between them and the massive animal as possible; it was never a good idea to tangle with a polar bear when its cubs were near. The wolves growled back at the bear, but happily moved away from the huge predator as well.

"Anyone here?" Crafter yelled as they neared the village.

The only sound was the crunching of their boots through the frozen crust of snow. The ever-present wind blew from the east, causing a jingling sort of sound to fill the air. Gameknight thought it sounded like delicate crystalline wind chimes, but he'd never heard that before in Minecraft.

"Looks like they're all gone," Hunter said.

"Come on," Gameknight said, sprinting forward.

The party ran across the frozen plane, the sound of twinkling wind chimes slowly getting louder. When they entered the village, the companions split up, searching the homes. Herder's wolves circled the cluster of buildings, smelling the ground for traces of NPCs, but quickly returned; they found nothing.

Gameknight stood next to the village well and waited, nervously shifting his bow from one hand to the other.

Squawk! Tux said.

Kneeling, the User-that-is-not-a-user patted his friend on the soft head. "I don't know where everyone is either. But if they're gone . . . where did they go?"

The penguin squawked again, then flopped over on her side and rolled about in the snow.

Hunter suddenly appeared at Gameknight's side, her unibrow furled in confusion.

"Anything?" he asked.

She shook her head, her curls bouncing about like crimson springs. "I didn't find anyone, but I found items from people's inventory discarded all over the place."

"That doesn't sound good," Gameknight replied. "Show me."

She led him to the nearest house. Right in front of the door, a pile of tools hovered just off the ground, bobbing up and down as if riding the gentle swells of an unseen ocean. The pickaxe, shovel and sword were covered with a thick layer of snow, making them difficult to see against the frozen ground.

"What are these?" he asked, pointing to the wall.

The sound of wind chimes grew louder.

Shards of ice were stuck into the wooden door. Each looked like a tiny dagger and was plunged deep into the wood. Gameknight reached out and touched the keen edge of a frozen spike; it was razor sharp. He glanced over his shoulder and found Crafter and Empech standing near the village well, talking. He motioned them to come near. Digger and Woodcutter saw the gesture and came as well.

"Anyone ever see anything like this before?" Gameknight asked, pointing to the door.

"Oh no," a high-pitched voice said. "Ice cores, yes, yes."

Gameknight turned and found Empech staring at the door, his eyes huge, a scared expression on his oversized, gray face.

"What?" Hunter asked. "Are these frozen spikey-things called ice cores?"

The pech shook his head, then glanced around nervously. The sound of the wind chimes grew louder, coming from south of the village. This drew the little gnome's attention away from the door and toward the jingling sound.

"They're coming," Empech screeched. He shifted nervously from foot to foot as if he were standing on blazing-hot coals. "Ice cores are coming. Can't you hear them?"

The wind chimes grew even louder, as if the source were now in the village.

"You mean those bell-like sounds?" Crafter said.

"Yes, yes, ice cores," the pech said, his deep blue eyes filled with fear. "They're coming. We must flee."

"Flee from what? A bunch of icicles clinking together?" Hunter asked.

Just then, a handful of razor sharp spikes of ice thudded against the wall of the home, one of them striking Gameknight in the shoulder. He flashed red, taking damage.

Turning, he drew his diamond sword to face the threat. Expecting skeletons or zombies or bears, Gameknight999 was shocked at what he saw. Weaving between the buildings were creatures he'd never seen before. Their heads looked as if they were made of packed snow and ice, a speckled blue and white texture to their faces, with black soulless eyes that stared right at Gameknight and his friends. Around their floating, disembodied heads, blue crystalline spikes revolved, each one faceted with razor-sharp edges and pointed tips, some of the icy shafts clinking together, making the wind chime sound.

The frozen spikes began spinning faster around one of the creatures, then it leaned forward and shot its armament at the company. Out of instinct, Gameknight reached into his inventory and drew his shield. Holding it before him, he felt the icy shards embed themselves into the rugged surface, some of them going all the way through and protruding out the back.

"I'm thinking we should get out of here," Hunter said urgently as she pulled a spike from her leg, grunting in pain.

"I think you're right," Gameknight replied.

The group turned to escape, but the sound of more wind chimes filled the air as another group of ice cores approached from the other side of the village. Mixed in with the floating terrors were creatures resembling armored guards, but as they neared, Gameknight saw they had no legs; the iron-clad monsters floated across the frozen ground just like the ice cores. A loud growl filled the air as a squat creature with white fur and frozen blue flesh ringing its mouth and eyes stepped around the corner of a building. Long, sharp teeth filled the creature's mouth, and its short muscular arms ended with dangerous-looking clawed hands. It bellowed again, causing the icy shards embedded in Gameknight's shield to vibrate like frozen tuning forks.

"Yeti!" Empech exclaimed in terror. "And aurora guards too. We are in trouble, yes, yes!"

They were surrounded, with their backs against the building. The ice cores spread out, getting ready to fire, as the yeti lifted a huge block of ice and prepared to throw it at the party. The aurora guards drew their steel swords, the light of the sun gleaming off the deadly, razor-sharp edges.

Gameknight knew if they tried to run through the crowd of approaching monsters, they would be doomed.

"Gameknight, what do we do?" Hunter asked "You have any plan that doesn't involve us being destroyed?"

But the User-that-is-not-a-user was overwhelmed with fear. He couldn't move. It felt as if his feet were frozen in the ground, and the blood in his veins had turned to ice. All Gameknight999 could do was stand there and wait for destruction to crash down upon them.

CHAPTER 7

BATTLE WITH ICE AND STEEL

Gameknight took a step backward, the fear of these strange wintery monsters nearly overwhelming. When he did, he bumped into the door and it slowly swung open, the frozen and rusty hinges screeching as if they'd been unused for a century.

"Good idea, Gameknight," Crafter said. "Everyone get inside the house."

They all piled inside, then slammed the door just as another barrage of ice spikes struck it, some of the deadly shards sticking all the way through the wood.

"Where's Herder?" Stitcher asked.

"He was patrolling the perimeter of the village with the wolves," Digger answered. "I hope he's going to be okay."

Gameknight glanced about the room, icicles of fear stabbing at his soul. Light from a torch on the wall reflected off the smooth, mirror-like blade of Woodcutter's axe, casting spots of illumination on the ceiling and walls. Empech stood far from the door, pacing back and forth as he muttered to himself, his voice too high-pitched and shrill to understand. Gameknight moved to his side.

"Empech, why are they attacking us?" Gameknight asked.

"They should not be here," the gnome said. "Servants of the Ice Queen, yes, yes. Very dangerous . . . very dangerous indeed."

"Those things are from the Twilight Forest?" Digger asked.

Squawk! Tux added.

Empech nodded his oversized head, his protruding lower jaw now quivering in fear.

"I remember when I was his captive, Entity303 said he'd done a lot of things to Minecraft," Weaver said. "He bragged about jumbling things up . . . maybe this is what he meant."

"I don't think it matters what he meant," Hunter snapped. "All that's important is how we get out of here."

"Hunter, be nice," Stitcher chided.

"Ahh . . . oh, sorry," the older sister said. "We're all just a little bit on edge."

More ice spikes struck the side of the home, making them all jump. To Gameknight, the sound of the frozen projectiles hitting the walls sounded like machine gun fire. It reminded him of a time he'd gone to play paintball with some friends. They had been trapped in a shed, with the only door covered by the enemy. Instead of charging out the front, Gameknight and his friends had slid under the wall from the back and had hidden behind the smoke generators. In an overwhelming victory, they'd taken the other players by surprise and gotten them all.

The wind chimes were even louder. More of the icy creatures were just outside the door.

"I know what we can do," the User-that-is-not-a-user said.

"What?" Crafter asked.

Gameknight moved to the door and opened it a crack, just enough to yell outside. "Herder, try to make some noise and draw them to the east."

He closed it quickly, just as a new group of deadly frozen shards embedded themselves into the wood. Tiny cracks spread across the door like fine spider's webs; it wasn't going to last long.

"You think he heard you?" Digger asked.

Squawk, squawk, the little penguin said nervously.

"I don't know, but we need to move regardless," Gameknight said. With a plan in his head, he felt his fear slowly slip away, replaced by all the pieces of his strategy. "Woodcutter, I need you to use your axe to make us another door, when I tell you."

The roar of a yeti shook the walls. Icy fists smashed against the door, making the boards creak and groan under the strain. The cracks grew deeper. Gameknight glanced at his companions and saw fear in their eyes.

"Digger, I need you to watch after Tux," the User-that-is-not-a-user said.

The stocky NPC nodded his head. He reached down and picked up Tux with his left hand, then moved to Woodcutter's side. Suddenly, a howl pierced through the yeti growls and the tinkling wind chime sounds of the ice cores.

"Good job, Herder," Gameknight said. "I knew I could count on you."

Weaver scowled and looked away.

"Woodcutter . . . NOW!" Gameknight said.

Woodcutter chopped through the wooden wall, carving up two of the blocks and making an opening.

"Go straight out and use the house for cover," Gameknight whispered.

The companions ran out of the structure, one after another, straight out into the frozen landscape. Gameknight waited for everyone to leave, then moved to the opening. Just as he was about to leave, the door behind him shattered. The hulking form of a yeti stepped into the room, the bellowing scream of the creature echoing across the land.

"Bye bye," Gameknight said, then placed blocks of cobblestone in the opening and sprinted away, leaving the creature pounding his fists on the gray cubes.

"Everyone, head back to the cobblestone platform!" Gameknight shouted to his friends. "Then we'll run for the library." He pulled his bow from his inventory and notched an arrow. "HERDER, HEAD FOR THE LIBRARY!"

A great roar came from behind. Turning around, he fired two quick shots, then sprinted away. He wasn't sure if his arrows had hit anything or not. Running as fast as he could, he caught up with the others, who had slowed to wait for him.

"Head for the bears," Gameknight said.

"You want to add *bears* to the party?" Hunter asked.

"Don't stop and dance with them," he replied. "Just run around them."

"Use the polar bears to slow our pursuers, yes, yes?" Empech said.

"Exactly."

As they ran, howls of excitement came from off to the right. Herder and his wolves were running parallel to their path, a huge army of ice cores and aurora guards in hot pursuit. For the first time, Gameknight could see the guards clearly. There were three types: one with a green helmet and chest plate, holding a shining steel sword, another wearing iron armor with a helmet that boasted two horns sticking out from either side and a silver chest plate, and the third wearing iron armor, but with a single hole in the middle of the helmet, as if it had just one giant eye. Each of the aurora guards had sparkling ice crystals and snowflakes falling out of their armor; the frozen debris seeming to hold them up in the air, for they had no legs. In fact, the monsters had no bodies, nor arms, nor faces . . . just armor and gleaming steel swords held at the ready.

A volley of frozen shards sprang into the air. The sunlight hit them as they arced high overhead, making the deadly projectiles sparkle like a cloud of jewels.

"Incoming!" Gameknight yelled.

He pulled out his shield and moved to Empech, holding it high over his head, protecting both himself and the gray-skinned pech. The spikes hit the shield, thudding like more machine gun fire.

"Everyone RUN!" Gameknight ordered.

They streaked across the snow with Herder and the wolves slowly edging closer. Glancing over his shoulder, Gameknight could see the ice cores had to wait until the icy shafts reappeared around their floating blue and white heads before firing again; at least they couldn't fire continuously.

How do you defeat those things? he thought. *I wish I'd watched more of the mod showcases about the Twilight Forest on YouTube. DireWolf20's videos would have really helped right about now.*

"Look out," Stitcher shouted.

While he'd been distracted thinking, Gameknight had slowed to a walk. A group of aurora guards were now closing in. Drawing his dual swords, the User-that-is-not-a-user waited for them to approach. The green armored guard attacked first, his steel sword flashing quickly in the bright sunlight. Reflected light hit Gameknight in the eyes and blinded him momentarily. Instinctively, he brought up his swords to defend himself. The steel blade crashed against his iron one, the impact jarring his arm. Swinging his diamond sword, Gameknight attacked where he thought the creature would be standing. A satisfying clank sounded when his sword found the aurora guard's helmet.

Suddenly, a loud shout cut through the air:

"WOODCUTTER!"

The tall NPC's battle cry echoed across the frozen land. He moved to Gameknight's side, his shining axe smashing into bright helmets and metal chest plates. The weapon flashed through the air like a streak of silver lightning, the mirror-like finish reflecting his victims just before the axe struck home. Where Woodcutter struck, Gameknight followed up with another attack, blocking the thrusts from the guards with his other blade. Working together, they quickly smashed the floating armor until all three monsters were destroyed.

Gameknight patted Woodcutter on the back and felt the cracks in his iron armor; the guards' steel swords had done some damage.

"Watch out!" Crafter shouted.

Pulling out his shield, he held it aloft, blocking the deadly frozen rain from striking them. More of the icy daggers stuck in his shield. Woodcutter used the blunt edge of his axe to dislodge the keen-edged shards, making the shield safer to hold.

"Thanks," the User-that-is-not-a-user said.

Woodcutter just smiled, then turned and ran as the ice cores renewed their frozen ammunition. A yeti lumbered forward, throwing a block of ice at Gameknight, but the User-that-is-not-a-user didn't wait around to see what would happen. He turned and sprinted after his friends. The block of ice hit the ground behind him and exploded, sending smaller cubes in all directions, but Gameknight was far enough away to escape harm.

"I see the library," Weaver shouted.

"Which way?" Gameknight replied.

"Between those two steep hills," the young boy said, pointing to the northwest.

Gameknight turned and saw two massive mounds of ice. They looked like a collection of ice spikes that had somehow merged together, forming a pair of huge, jagged hills. Past the glacial blue mountains, the cobblestone library was just barely visible in the distance.

They used every bit of speed they had left, running for the two hills and the structure beyond. Herder and his wolves had now caught up with the party, the lanky boy running next to Crafter.

"Wolves . . . delay!" Herder yelled.

The wolves peeled away from the formation, and darted between the ice cores, aurora guards, and yetis, nipping at legs and arms, distracting the monsters. It gave the villagers a little breathing room, allowing their lead to grow.

As they neared the hills, Gameknight had an idea. He pulled out a stack of wood from his inventory. Slowing, he stopped, then began placing the blocks across the gap between the two icy hills.

"Herder, recall the wolves," the User-that-is-not-a-user commanded.

The boy put his stubby fingers to his mouth and whistled. The creatures instantly disengaged from the monsters and sprinted for their position.

"What good are those blocks of wood gonna do?" Hunter asked. "They'll just jump over them."

Gameknight placed more wood on the ground, then pulled out flint and steel. Carefully, he lit the wood, and the flames instantly melted the snow on the ground around them. He left a gap for the wolves to get by without getting burned. Once the last of the animals had passed, he sealed the opening and filled it with more burning wood.

"All of those monsters are from the Ice Queen's castle," Gameknight said. "I bet they don't like fire very much."

Hunter smiled and nodded her head.

They ran to the other end of the pass between the frozen mounds and placed more blocks of wood, lighting them as well. Gameknight smiled with pride at his cleverness, then turned and headed for the library.

When they entered the dusty room, they found the normal cobwebs hanging in the corners, the old, multi-colored books lining the shelves, and a thick layer of dust on everything except for the footprints that already marked the floor. The slanted writing bench stood in the corner of the room, with ancient-looking rune-covered pages sitting on the wooden surface.

"It seems our enemy found what he was looking for?" Woodcutter said, pointing to the empty space on the table.

Looking closer, Gameknight realized one of the pages was missing.

"Maybe you're right," he replied as he reached down and picked up the book Entity303 had crafted.

The sound of wind chimes grew louder as they monsters begin to get through the fires the group had set, but they were abruptly cut off by an explosion. Through the doorway, they could see balls of fire streaking through the air and striking the monsters that approached. . . strange. Yetis hollered in pain as the clanking sound of aurora guard armor being shattered filled the air.

"What's shooting those fireballs?" Crafter asked.

"Who cares?" Hunter replied.

"The enemy of my enemy is my friend?" Gameknight asked, wondering what was going on outside.

Hunter nodded her head, then stepped closer to Gameknight999.

"Let's get out of here," she said.

The User-that-is-not-a-user nodded, then waited for everyone to gather close. Weaver stood next to Herder and scowled, then moved so he was standing next to Crafter instead.

"Everyone ready to head to the next Age?" Gameknight asked.

They nodded.

He concentrated on the book and imagined clicking it, and suddenly was enveloped in colorful mist. As they disappeared, Gameknight thought he heard something call out in a deep voice:

"I willll catch youuuu yet, annnnd willll feast on youuuuur maaagic."

But before he could identify who had said it, they were gone.

CHAPTER 8

ENTITY303 RETURNS

Entity303 stepped out of the dark tunnel that led from the massive caves and moved into a shadowy forest. The sun was high in the air, but the thick branches and leaves overhead allowed very little light to reach the ground. Through some of the few gaps in the foliage, he could see the sun's face; it was black as coal, like a hole in the sky with the eternal darkness of the void showing through. A shadowy corona surrounded the object, giving it a strange square halo. Even though the normally blinding solar body was dark, the light shining down upon the land was still bright. The sky, barely visible through the treetops, was a sickly, pale green, like the color of poisoned flesh . . . it was wonderful!

Some clouds moved across the sky, blocking the sun momentarily. It brought Entity303's attention away from the environment and back to the job at hand.

"Those pathetic cave-dwellers down there in the darkness stink like garbage," Entity303 said to himself. "I think the males, the Glugs, smell the worst, but the females, the Mogs, are pretty terrible as well. How can any creature live like that? Ugh, they deserve their suffering." He slowly lowered his sword and glared at the tunnel opening, the hulking creatures in the rocky passage below now choosing to retreat instead of attacking him in the forest. "I'm just glad I was able to make many of them suffer a bit more."

He glanced at his yellow-glowing blade and smiled viciously, then looked around to see if anyone was nearby; he was alone. Putting the blade back into his inventory, he moved away from the tunnel that led out of the caves and walked across the forest floor.

"If I hadn't found that missing page, I would have never been able to come back to this Age." He truly loved the sound of his own voice. "Finding it in that frozen world was a stroke of luck. It could have taken hundreds of Ages until I found the Cave World page I needed."

He smiled at his cleverness, but was sorry there weren't others there to recognize his brilliance. Walking further away from the dark tunnel, Entity303 moved deeper into the forest and gazed upward. Massive trees stretched thirty blocks into the air, if not higher. The ground was completely bare; just brown, lifeless dirt. There was once a time when it had been covered with deep red grass, blood-grass as it was called. But that had been before the genocide . . . before the ruler of this land, King Iago, had destroyed the ridiculous fire-imps that fed on the crimson plants.

It made Entity303 laugh to recall it. The king was so proud of his victory over the tiny fire-imps, but it had actually all been the user's own idea. By destroying those little creatures, it freed up Iago's workforce to do Entity303's bidding.

Suddenly, a cloud in the sky moved just a bit, allowing rays of sunlight to penetrate the leafy roof and fall to the forest floor. It looked like shafts of liquid gold being cast down from the heavens, some of the light falling upon a pile of food lying on the ground.

There were no animals to be seen anywhere, no sources of food for the cave-dwellers that groveled like filthy creatures in the shadowy depths. Only the meager crops they could grow in the darkness underground were available to them . . . and that was not enough for all of them to survive. The rest of the food necessary for the subterranean creatures to live was found in these piles lying innocently on the forest floor. Thin strands of the finest spider silk ran up from the ground near the edge of the mounds of fruits and breads and cakes, invisible to the untrained eye.

Entity303 walked up to one pile. Moving around the food, he looked for the threads that he knew were there, waiting to get to the right angle so the few rays of sunlight that pierced through the leaves and branches would reflect off the fine lines.

"There you are," he said as the silk thread lit up silver. Grasping the thread firmly, he gave it a tug. "Pull me up, you fools!"

Shapes moved through the leaves high overhead. They were too far away to see clearly, but Entity303 knew they were up there. He'd been to this Age many times, and knew everything about it; this was his home in Minecraft, and he owned every bit, even though the king and the other inhabitants likely would not agree.

"Hurry up before I use a couple of fire-arrows on that tree!" Entity303 yelled up into the trees.

Suddenly, the user was pulled upward, caught in the net that had been hidden under the pile of food now dangling below him. He was pulled through a hole in the leaves and landed in a small corral, a high wooden fence marking the edges. The bright sunlight that shined down upon the treetops shocked him at first, but once his eyes adjusted, he saw tree-dwellers standing about. One of them moved forward and peered through the slats of the fence while others walked about across the treetops, performing errands for some rich benefactor.

"Open the gate now, or I'll break it down and destroy all of you!" Entity303 snapped.

Instantly, the gate opened and his jailer stepped back away from the user. The others on the leafy roof stopped what they were doing and moved back as well, cowering in silence.

"That's better. Now tell your king that Entity303 has returned to complete our bargain. I have what he wants, and he had better be ready for me, or someone's gonna suffer. I don't have time to be delayed by just a bunch of useless tree-dwellers."

They murmured to each other momentarily and then went about their business. One of them stepped forward. He was wearing a wrinkled and torn smock that was at one time a deep forest-green, but now was stained and worn out. Decorative stitching had adorned the front and sleeves, but those colorful threads had fallen off long ago, leaving behind a few threadbare traces.

The disheveled tree-dweller, just like everyone moving about on the treetops, wore a mask that completely covered their face and head, each a different color and decoration. The one standing before Entity303 wore a mask colored sky blue, but it was scratched and cracked here and there. Smudges of dirt and tree sap could be seen on the sides and back. Things at one time had been glued to the mask—Entity303 assumed it had been gems—but they were gone now, leaving only slight discolorations where they had once sat.

"You look pathetic, have you no pride?" Entity303 said. "Your clothing and mask are the worst. Someone that looks as bad as you must be useless. I'm not surprised you've been sentenced to be a tree-dweller instead of living up there." He pointed up into the sky at the islands of stone and dirt that floated high overhead, the colorful homes and buildings on the islands glistening with elegance. "You were obviously not worthy of being a sky-dweller, so now you live in the trees." He raised his voice. "YOU'RE ALL PATHETIC!"

Many of the tree-dwellers glared at Entity303 through their filthy masks, their eyes glowing with a silvery light as they struggled to contain their anger. He smiled. None of these wretched creatures were brave enough to attack . . . they were almost the lowest of the low. The only things more pathetic were fallen-knights.

He turned back to the one with the sky-blue mask.

"I should put you out of your misery," the user growled.

He heard a sniffle from behind the mask and could tell the tree-dweller was crying . . . how pitiful. In a single fluid motion, Entity303 drew his sword, the glowing yellow blade casting a warm light on the top of the tree. The masked tree-dweller took a step back, probably afraid, but Entity303 couldn't tell . . . the dweller's mask hid any emotions, which was one of its purposes. Disgusted with their cowardice, he put away his sword.

"I won't talk with this . . . thing," Entity303 said to the disheveled tree-dweller, then raised his voice. "Bring me the Overseer!"

The green clad tree-dweller quickly ran across the treetops, looking for the Overseer, or maybe just running away.

Another NPC stepped forward, this one wearing chocolate-brown smock. It stretched from chin to ankle, and their hands were covered with black gloves. Instantly, Entity303 could tell it was a woman; it was something about the way she walked. Fine lines of red and pink were woven into the smock, carving out broad curving patterns across the front and back. In places, the threads were missing and had not been replaced, showing the lack of care this tree-dweller had for her appearance.

On her face, she wore a mask that at one time had been pristine white with lines of gold painted in intricate designs across the front and sides. The mask wrapped all the way around her face, hiding her hair and skin. But this mask no longer shone with the luster of sophistication and wealth. Now, it was just old. The gold lines had flaked off and the pure white color had faded to that of a stained almost pale yellow. Obviously she didn't care about keeping her appearances up; that was why she and all the others were sentenced to being tree-dwellers by the king. All of society in this world was determined by wealth and appearance, and those too poor or lazy to make themselves look presentable did not deserve to live in the comfort of the sky islands, according to the king.

"A message is being sent to King Iago," the white-masked tree-dweller said. "When we receive a message from the King, you will be escorted to the grand palace."

"I'll just go there now!" Entity303 replied.

The villager stepped forward to protest, but the user waved his sword with lightning speed, the yellow light from the weapon illuminating the treetop as if it were ablaze. The masked NPC wisely stepped back and allowed the Entity303 to pass.

He walked across the green, leafy carpet, looking for a place where he could go up to the sky islands over-head. With the branches of these trees being so wide, it was easy to walk from one tree to the next without the threat of a fatal fall all the way to the ground below.

Pushing aside curious tree-dwellers who tried to befriend him in hopes of raising their station in soci-ety, he walked across the treetops until he finally saw what he sought. Built out of green-stained clay so as to blend into the treetops was a structure that stood tall and proud. Four broad pillars stretched up to a domed roof whose curve was perfectly hemispherical. A hole three blocks in radius was cut into the exact center of the dome.

Entity303 moved to a set of stairs carved into the foliage of the tree and climbed up to the clay platform that sat under the dome. He looked up through the hole in the roof. High overhead, sky islands floated in the air, some very large and supporting multiple buildings while others were smaller, only able to hold a single home. Each structure was uniquely decorated with gold and emeralds and diamonds and obsidian and quartz, the expense of the decorations matching each owner's power in the society.

The architecture of each was completely different, each more extravagant than the next. Conical roofs of lapis stretched high into the sky on some; tall spires of red and blue clay jutted into the air, supporting stained glass roofs; colorful waterfalls fell from the top of buildings into calm pools with fountains shooting streams of the blue liquid into the air. It was like a sampling of every building technique possible in Minecraft. But one thing they all had in common: each had softly glowing yellow blocks beneath the island. These were levitation blocks, and the cubes were critical to the safety of every floating island. Strange green creatures crawled around beneath the islands, tending to the blocks, making sure they were always fueled and working.

Entity303 looked at the ground and found a dull brown block, the dome's opening directly overhead. The cube stood out against the nearly constant field of green that spread out across the treetops. Glowing lines crisscrossed the face of the cube like a tangled spider's web, the orange light from the cube gently lighting the space under the domed roof. The cube reminded him of magma blocks, but of course did not burn when touched. It was a catapult block: exactly what Entity303 was looking for.

Reaching up, the user removed his white furry Alpha Yeti chest plate and placed it in his inventory. He then pulled out a set of Elytra wings and strapped them to his back.

"The king has instructed you to wait here," one of the masked villagers said.

This one wore a nicer mask; he was likely the Overseer of the tree-dwellers. His mask was a dark blue that at one time had small emeralds across the front and side. Only a few of the gems remained, most either sold or had fallen off from disrepair. At one point, it looked as if there had been intricate lines of yellow painted along the sides, but those too, like the emeralds, had chipped away from careless use. Their smock was a dirty red that had probably been bright at one time, but now it was dull, like red paint mixed with too much dirty water. It was pathetic.

"Look at your mask and clothes," Entity303 said, gesturing toward the disheveled person. "I'm afraid if I speak to you, some of your filth may rub off onto me. Step back."

The tree-dweller tensed, his eyes filling with the silvery rage he'd seen before. The villager took a step forward, but didn't reach for his blade.

Fool, Entity303 thought.

Spinning, he drew his blade and struck the Overseer before the tree-dweller could shout out. Entity303 hit him again and again until he disappeared with a pop, leaving behind glowing balls of XP and his pathetic excuse for a mask. The user stepped forward and allowed the XP to flow into him, then kicked the mask across the leafy rooftop, where it fell through a hole and plummeted to the ground.

"Let that be a lesson to you cowardly tree-dwellers," Entity303 shouted to the onlookers. "All of you answer to me. If any of you disagree, step forward now and show that you aren't a spineless sheep." None of the tree-dwellers moved, their stained and scratched masks slowly lowering to look at the ground. "I thought so."

He laughed, then stepped on the catapult block. Instantly, it shot him up into the air. As he climbed, the user leaned forward, causing his wings to snap open. Bending this way and that, Entity303 soared higher and higher, flying toward the massive floating island above him.

His wings trembled under the force of the wind, but he knew they would not be destroyed; he'd put a *Mending* enchantment on them long ago. He didn't really need the wings to get to the sky island, because the catapult block would shoot him straight up onto the structure.

But he didn't want to arrive just like everyone else—no, Entity303 wanted to arrive in style . . . like royalty.

With his wings outstretched, he did complicated loops and turns, knowing full well those on the sky island were watching him. Other people flew in the air, most just gliding from island to island; it was how they traveled between the sky islands. But none of the sky-dwellers came near him; they knew how to mind their own business.

Banking to the left, Entity303 aimed for the massive palace that sat on the largest of the islands. Built of white quartz, gold, and blue lapis, the structure was obscene in its opulence. Gilded towers climbed to the sky, ornately decorated walls ringed the structure and delicately stained glass cast bright colors on the ground as the light from the waning sun shone through the openings. It was a spectacular construction, built by workers that suffered terrible brutalities while working on it, then were likely cast off the island when the palace was complete. Entity303 loved it.

Trading speed for altitude, he climbed higher into the air, well above the cloud layer, then dove straight down. He shot through the sky like a magical bullet, his armor and wings shimmering with magical enchantments. He sped over the high wall that ringed the palace and streaked toward the king's private courtyard. Pulling up at the last possible instant, he landed gracefully on a flawless circle of blood-red grass.

Entity303 quickly removed his wings, and replaced them with his Alpha Yeti armor. With his sword drawn, he approached a villager dressed in a royal purple smock, the edges trimmed with gold thread. Delicate patterns were stitched into the garment, with diamonds and emeralds attached here and there.

The ruler sparkled like a firework show. He stood as Entity303 approached. Two of his guards, both dressed in all black and wearing white masks and white gloves, moved to stand before their king. Delicate stitchings of white and gold adorned their shadowy smocks, the white on black making them almost appear as skeletons in the shadow of the afternoon sun. King Iago held out his hands, signaling the guards to stand down and lower their golden swords.

"My friend, you have returned," Iago said from behind his mask.

The mask was made of solid gold, but as he neared, Entity303 could see runes sketched across its surface; they reminded him of those he'd recently seen in the Rune Dungeons under the White Castle. It had the smallest of gems attached to the front and side, almost too small to see, but when the sun hit them they sparkled like tiny little exploding stars. The mask was magnificent, a work of art that took his breath away for an instant.

"Welcome, Entity303," Iago said. "You have been away for a long time. It's good to have you home. All is nearly ready for you. Soon, we can finish our bargain and each can go our separate way."

Entity303 laughed. He knew what was going to happen to this world, and all of the other worlds, when his plan was complete.

"Yes, indeed," Entity303 said with an evil smirk. "We can go our separate ways."

He laughed a vile, malicious laugh that made the illustrious ruler cringe.

Soon, my revenge will be complete, Entity303 thought, *and all of Minecraft will be destroyed, including this idiot of a king and those fools who still follow. Nothing can stop me now!*

CHAPTER 9

WORLD OF DARKNESS

The water was frigid; it made his feet numb, and from there the cold seemed to seep up throughout his body, chilling him to the very center of his being. Gameknight999 had appeared in a dark world, materializing on a square platform of cobblestone five blocks by five blocks in size. A single torch, as always, lit the stone landing pad, but everything around them had been cloaked in darkness.

Gameknight had been the first to step off the platform, landing knee deep in water. Now the rest of the party was following him, looking for anything solid to get under their feet.

"You don't suppose this was what Entity303 was looking for, do you?" Crafter asked. "A water world?"

"I don't know," Gameknight replied.

"If you did, you probably wouldn't tell us all anyway," Weaver grumbled under his breath, loud enough that everyone heard.

The User-that-is-not-a-user sighed. Weaver's anger toward him made Gameknight sad, but he knew keeping certain details from him about the future was necessary, even though it was difficult.

A faint light shone in the darkness. Gameknight headed to it, hoping it was a way out. As the party neared, it seemed as if the light was more like a cluster of lights hanging at the end of green lines. Finally, when they reached the illumination source, they found glowing berries attached to vines hanging down from what looked like a ceiling.

"Torch berries, yes, yes," Empech said. "Can be fed to the Moonworm Queen." The little pech reached up and plucked the lowest cluster of berries from the green strands and stuffed them into his oversized backpack.

"Hey, there's a wall over here," Stitcher shouted, her voice echoing into the darkness.

The young girl placed a torch on the stone wall. Instantly, a circle of light burst into existence, painting a yellow glow on the surroundings.

"Over here is solid ground," Digger said near the edge of the circle of light. They moved toward the stocky NPC as he climbed out of the water and placed another torch on the ground.

"It looks like we're in some kind of massive cave," Woodcutter said.

The tall NPC moved to Digger's side and held his hands momentarily over the torch, warming them ever so slightly. He then carefully climbed a nearby stony hill.

"I can see things glowing in the distance," Woodcutter said. "They look like some kind of colorful mushrooms."

"Glowshrooms, yes, yes," Empech said. "They began growing in the dark places of Minecraft when things started to deteriorate."

Gameknight climbed the hill and stood next to Woodcutter. Gazing out into the darkness, he saw multicolored lights illuminating small patches of ground. They looked like decorative pink and yellow and green candies on a black velvet cloth. Near the glowshrooms, Gameknight thought he saw something like wheat, but that made no sense. Why would someone want to grow wheat in a cave?

"I like the glowshrooms," Stitcher said when she reached Woodcutter's side. "They're pretty."

"Pretty?" Weaver asked.

She started to reply, then fell silent when the sound of footsteps echoed off the stone walls. They all became deathly quiet and listened to the darkness. More footsteps shuffled through the shadows . . . a lot of them.

"Who's there?" Gameknight shouted as he drew his enchanted sword, the glowing weapon throwing out a splash of iridescent purple light around them. "What do you want?"

More footsteps shuffled through the darkness, but this time they were accompanied by grunts and growls; the sounds of monsters. Gameknight's imagination went wild with speculation; was it zombies, or maybe yetis, or even those terrifying ice cores? His mind whirred through the possibilities, making it difficult to think.

"I think we need to keep moving instead of just standing around," Hunter said quietly, snapping the User-that-is-not-a-user out of his trance. "A moving target is harder to hit."

"Okay, it's your idea. Which way do we go?" Gameknight asked, his voice shaking.

"I'd say toward the glowing mushroom thingies," she replied.

"OK, I'll lead with the Moonworm Queen," the User-that-is-not-a-user said.

Gameknight reached into his inventory and withdrew what looked like a large beetle with a brightly glowing yellow body. He'd found it in the Twilight Forest while trying to save Weaver, and it had proven useful throughout their adventures. The Queen had the unique ability to spit out glowing worms, called moonworms, that could adhere to any solid surface. The wriggling insects would act like a fluorescent green torch and give off light, something they desperately needed right now.

The creature wrapped its six legs around Gameknight's wrist as if it were used to being there, and waited. With the glowing worm in his left hand, and enchanted sword in his right, Gameknight headed for the glowshrooms in the distance. He sparingly placed moonworms on the ground, still unsure how many the queen had left inside her bulbous, radiant body.

"Wolves . . . protect," Herder said.

Ghostly white shapes disappeared into the darkness, forming a ring around the companions. At times, their eyes could be seen reflecting the faint light from the glowing worms, but for the most part, they were completely invisible.

Footsteps shuffled overhead, followed by the sound of a block of gravel falling to the ground.

"What was that?" Digger asked, his voice shaking.

Squawk, Tux said softly.

Digger patted the little penguin softly on the head.

"Just keep going," Crafter said. "It was probably nothing."

They all could tell he was lying to make them feel better.

"Do not fear. Empech thinks the caves are safe," the little gnome said in his high-pitched squeaky voice.

Deep growls floated out of the darkness from behind.

"Move faster . . . they're right behind us!" Digger exclaimed.

A deep, guttural moan echoed from the darkness.

"Digger's right, let's get moving," Weaver said desperately.

"I think you're right," Gameknight answered and started to run.

Hunter turned with her bow drawn, ready to fire into the darkness, but the little gnome put a calming hand on her arm.

"Do not shoot," Empech said. "It will be alright, yes, yes."

Hunter looked at the pech, a confused expression on her square face, then lowered her weapon.

Gameknight streaked across the stone, placing moonworms only where necessary. As they drew nearer to the glowing mushrooms, Gameknight saw there was indeed a small field of wheat struggling to grow in the faint pink light. The stalks of wheat looked pale and crooked, as if barely alive; the amount of light was insufficient. Gameknight placed a moonworm next to the plot, giving it a bit more light, then dashed past, heading for the next cluster of glowing fungi.

They followed a steep wall as the sound of shuffling feet filled the air behind them. There were more creatures following them now . . . a lot more. Sharp claws clicked and scratched the hard, stone floor; it sounded like Gameknight's cat, Tiger, walking across the kitchen tile when his claws were too long. It was an eerie sound that made his spine cringe with fear.

They came to the next glowshroom and found another small farm. Gameknight fired two moonworms at the ground on either side of the field, this one filled with beetroot. As he sped past, Gameknight could see the plants were pale and withered in the dim lighting, but were able to grow, though barely.

Sounds of pursuit grew louder, the grunts and growls coming at them from all sides.

"I think they're closing in on us," Hunter said.

"Faster . . . go faster," Digger said, his deep voice booming off the walls.

The companions sped their way through the cave until they finally found what looked like a tunnel. It led upward out of the massive cavern. None of them really cared where it went, as long as it took them out of this terrifying place.

Gameknight led them into the passage, placing the moonworms on the walls and ceiling. The wolves behind him growled. Glancing over his shoulder, the User-that-is-not-a-user saw a massive horde of monsters entering the passage. They were big creatures with two large teeth that could almost be described as tusks sticking out of their mouths. Their green skin looked like that of a zombie, but without the decaying wounds and loose pieces of flesh hanging off their arms or chests. Some of the monsters were now climbing along the walls and ceiling, long black claws digging into the stone and holding them in place. The pursuing horde was moving faster, leaping up the steep slope as if gravity didn't fully apply to them.

"They're getting closer," Digger said, his voice shaking.

"I know, just keep going," Gameknight shouted.

I wish I had some TNT right now, he thought.

Glancing at Weaver, he saw the young boy was sweating, partly from the exertion and partly from fear. The NPC glanced back at Gameknight and glared, his anger painted vividly on his face.

"There's an opening ahead!" Herder said.

The lanky boy was near the head of the formation now, his long legs allowing him to go faster than the others. His wolves howled triumphantly.

"It's the surface!" Stitcher yelled, the red light of dusk filling the opening with hues of red and orange.

She shot out of the tunnel, then stopped and drew her bow. Gameknight ran for the opening as he watched Stitcher place blocks under her so she could shoot at the subterranean creatures if they continued their pursuit. Hunter reached her side and did the same, constructing her own archer tower as she waited. The rest of the company reached the opening and found themselves in a huge forest, the trees impossibly tall with no branches near the ground.

"They aren't following us," Stitcher said.

Gameknight turned and stared down into the tunnel. The monsters had stopped and milled about far from the opening. It was as if they were afraid to go to the surface.

"Why did they stop?" Crafter asked.

"Maybe they're afraid of something," Hunter said.

"All of those monsters are afraid of something up there?" Woodcutter said. "Maybe we should be afraid as well."

Gameknight nodded his head, then turned to survey the landscape. The sun was slowly setting in the west, but there was something strange about it. The colors along the horizon, bands of red and orange, seemed normal, but for some reason, the face of the sun was black. Maybe a cloud was blocking the sun . . . strange. Dusk splashed crimson light across the forest, bathing everything with an eerie red glow. It made the monsters in the mouth of the tunnel seem all the more terrifying, if that was even possible.

The forest stretched out in all directions with bare dirt covering the ground. There wasn't the faintest scrap of grass or bushes or flowers or anything . . . just trees, tall tall trees and a barren forest floor. It was a strange setting and felt violently unnatural.

Suddenly, Gameknight had the sensation there were eyes watching him, a lot of eyes, and it felt as if they were unfriendly eyes, expecting them to do something . . . but what were they waiting for?

CHAPTER 10

FLOATING ISLANDS

With the wolves spread out around them, the intrepid explorers moved away from the clot of green, muscular bodies that filled the tunnel opening. The monsters growled and moaned and muttered at Gameknight and his friends, but with all of them making deep, guttural sounds at the same time, it was difficult to determine if they were speaking to them or just making angry noises at the meal that had gotten away.

"Are they following?" Digger asked, his voice weak with fear.

Hunter glanced over her shoulder; the opening to the tunnel remained empty.

"No, it looks like the creatures went back into the cave . . . for now, anyway," she said.

Breathing a sigh of relief, the User-that-is-not-a-user finally relaxed. The muscles in his shoulders and neck were sore from being tense for what seemed like an endless time in the dark caves. They moved through the forest, more for the sake of being away from those creatures than to get anywhere. The forest was as dark as a moonless night, though the silvery lunar face was still rising up away from the eastern horizon. But with the thick roof of leaves and branches overhead, only the occasional beam of moonlight managed to make it to the forest floor.

"What were those things?" Crafter asked. "Empech, do you know anything about those creatures?"

"The inhabitants of the caves were not dangerous, yes, yes," the little gnome said.

"Not dangerous?!" Digger exclaimed, shocked. "Didn't you see those long black claws and terrible teeth?"

"They indeed looked ferocious and strong, but they were not enemies," the pech said. "Empech could sense it, yes, yes. They are a peaceful people."

"Peaceful? Hah!" Digger replied in disbelief, then slowed from running to walking, the rest of the party following his lead.

"They did not pursue," Empech pointed out as he adjusted the straps of his huge backpack.

"Maybe there's something in this forest to make those creatures afraid," Stitcher said.

"My sister's right," Hunter said as she passed through one of the rare moonbeams, the silvery light illuminating her crimson curls and making them burst with color. "There must be something nasty out here in this forest. Less talking and more watching."

The villagers nodded then turned their heads, scanning the forest.

"We need to find a defendable place to wait until sunrise," Crafter said.

"You're right," Gameknight replied.

"What about those trees over there?" Woodcutter said quietly, pointing with his axe.

Off to the right was a cluster of trees grouped close together, their branches high overhead merging together into the continuous canopy of wood and leaves. The copse of trees stood on the edge of a small clearing bathed in moonlight.

"Herder, have a wolf check it out," Gameknight said quietly.

The lanky boy pulled long strands of dark hair from his face and pointed. The pack leader shot through the forest, its white fur appearing almost gray in the dim lighting. But when the creature darted through the clearing, the wolf seemed to glow as if enchanted, its fur sparkling in the moonlight. It sprinted through the clearing, then reached the cluster of trees. After sniffing the ground and searching the surroundings, the majestic creature gave off a single, staccato bark.

"It's OK," Herder said, pride showing on his face.

"You do a great job with your wolves," the User-that-is-not-a-user said. "I'm really proud of you."

"Thanks, Gameknight," the lanky boy replied. "They're my friends, just like all of you are." Herder smiled. Clearly he enjoyed the praise from his idol and friend.

"Maybe we should stop this mutual admiration session and get somewhere safe," Weaver growled.

The boy flashed an angry scowl at Herder, then glared at Gameknight999 with such a venomous stare, it almost hurt.

"Weaver, we aren't a mutual admir . . ."

But the young boy didn't listen. Instead, he turned and ran through the forest, toward the cluster of trees. Gameknight sighed and watched as the boy sprinted around tree trunks and across the bright clearing.

"You're really good with people," Hunter said with a smile and slapped him on the back, then followed the boy toward the cluster of trees.

"Don't worry, Gameknight, Weaver will eventually come to terms with what has transpired," Crafter said. "He'll eventually realize you had to lie to him in the past, and you can't tell him everything now because of the past . . . and the future. Eventually he'll understand."

"But did you see how he looked at me?" the User-that-is-not-a-user said in a low voice. "He hates me."

Gameknight started walking toward the cluster of trees while the others ran.

"How can I ever convince him to forgive me?"

"Time heals all wounds," Crafter replied. "Just be patient."

The two friends walked toward the clearing. When Gameknight stepped into the moonlight, he glanced at the dirt. Square sections of wood were visible on the ground, each one covered with a thin layer of dust and the occasional stray leaf. Stopping in the middle, he scanned the forest floor and found more of the wooden ruins, some of them in an "L" shape while others were large rectangles.

There used to be a village here, he thought. *What happened to it? It's as if it's been erased from the surface of this world.*

"Crafter, come see something interesting," Gameknight called out .

The young NPC moved to his side. The moonlight lit his short blond hair as if it were spun from gold.

"Look at the . . ." Before Gameknight could finish he saw Crafter looking into the sky, his stubby finger pointing upward, a look of awe filling his bright blue eyes.

The User-that-is-not-a-user glanced up and was shocked. Huge islands of stone and dirt floated high in the air, tall trees on the islands stretching up even higher. The floating lands were covered with bright red grass, the leaves on the trees a sparkling silver. Each island had a structure built on it using exotic materials and rare gemstone blocks.

As he moved through the clearing to get a better view of the many islands and structures, Gameknight noticed that every construction was different and more magnificent than the next. It was as if they held a building contest up there, and points were given for the most spectacular features and decorations.

People moved about on the sky islands, some of them jumping off the edge and soaring to a nearby land, gliding through the air using what looked like gray wings strapped to their backs. Gameknight knew these were Elytra wings, something that had been added to Minecraft in the Combat Update, version 1.9. Gameknight moved through the clearing, looking up toward the next island coming into view. When he reached the far edge of the opening in the forest roof, he saw something that took his breath away.

A huge floating island, much larger than the others, hovered high in the sky. Tall trees bordered the edge of the land, but at the center, a gigantic palace made of white and gold loomed high over the other sky islands. The castle had a majestic look to it, as if it were the seat of power or the center of this universe.

Beneath the sky island, creatures crawled about, doing something to the yellow-glowing blocks that lined the underside. Suddenly, one of the creatures lost its grip and fell. Its deep, guttural scream echoed across the land as it plummeted to the forest below.

"You better open your Elytra, quick," Gameknight muttered, but then he saw the creature had none.

The doomed soul suddenly became silent. The User-that-is-not-a-user imagined the terror that must have gone through the creature's mind and was sad, and at the same time angry.

Every one of those workers should have had a pair of Elytra wings for safety. What are they thinking?!

He looked back to the massive floating island and the huge structure that dominated the sky. Something about it seemed sinister and evil. Sharp corners and narrow spikes of glass stuck up here and there, making the thing sparkle in the moonlight, but also appear dangerous.

And in that instant, Gameknight knew where his enemy was heading.

"That's where Entity303 is going," Gameknight said, pointing up at the gigantic thing.

"How can you know that for certain?" Crafter asked. "He could be anywhere in this strange land."

"Gameknight999 is correct, yes, yes. Empech can feel something evil on those floating clouds of grass and trees." Empech moved to Crafter's side and looked up at the huge castle. "There is something up there that is an affront to Minecraft. Entity303 will be drawn to that evil like a butterfly to a flower."

"Yeah, but he's an evil butterfly," Hunter added with a smile, "and that's one huge flower."

They all laughed except Gameknight999.

"I think we should build some defenses here between these trees," Crafter said as he pulled out a stack of wood and started placing them on the ground.

"No," Gameknight said.

"No?" the others echoed.

The User-that-is-not-a-user shook his head.

"For some reason, I think we need to be invisible here," he explained. "Instead of building walls, we need to dig a hidey-hole in the ground, then seal it over our heads."

"Things cannot attack what cannot be seen, yes, yes," Empech said.

The others nodded, then pulled out shovels and pickaxes and started to dig.

Gameknight stared up at that floating island and knew they had to go up there, somehow, but he had no idea how. And, worse, he had no idea what Entity303 had waiting for them up there, but he knew it wouldn't be good.

CHAPTER 11

THE DEMON STALKS HIS PREY

Kahn walked through the dark cave, the thick claw at the end of his leather wing scraping against the stone wall.

"I caaan feel that magical gnome," he growled to himself, his words long and drawn out, "but I lost track of themmm in this currrsed cave."

His eyesight in the darkness was good, but the weak villagers disappeared into a passage that led to the surface before he'd caught up to them. A massive group of cave-dwellers now still stood within that tunnel, making it difficult to follow his prey and emerge from the subterranean world unnoticed.

"I could dessstroy all of thossse creaturrres," Kahn grumbled to himself, "but they will draaaw attentionnn to meee. That is somethinggg I do not wannnt . . . for nowww."

He flapped his great leathery wings and moved up to the ceiling. Digging his long dark claws into the stone, he clung to the ceiling and waited for the monsters to exit the tunnel and return to their underground world. Slowly, the creatures stopped muttering warnings to those that escaped and retreated from the passage. They moved back into the darkness, toward their sad homes.

With his magical abilities, Kahn could feel their hunger; these green creatures were slowly starving and wanted to go to the surface in search of food, but they were afraid of something. And that fear was more powerful than the starvation gnawing away at their bodies.

How strrrange that mussst be . . . to be afffraid, the demon thought, amused.

When the last of the creatures retreated into the darkness, Kahn released his grip on the cave's rocky wall and dropped to the ground. He walked to the tunnel, his long legs moving him quickly across the uneven surface.

The tunnel was low and narrow. Pulling in his dark wings, the demon lowered his head and stooped so the long white horns that protruded from his head would not scrape against the ceiling. Hunched over, Kahn walked through a narrow passage, his clawed feet scratching on the stone. Ahead, he could see the opening to the world above, though it was nearly as dark as this subterranean universe. Crouching even lower so as to avoid a group of stones hanging down from the ceiling, he ran through the passage, anxious to get out into the open again.

When he reached the opening, Kahn leapt into the air and flapped his huge shadowy wings. They bit into the wind and pulled him high into the sky. He climbed near the treetops but sensed danger in the foliage; there was something hiding amongst the branches and leaves. The demon considered flying through the green leaves and just destroying whatever hid up there, but he was more interested in the magical creature and his servants. For now, he would wait and remain unseen . . . there was always time to destroy later.

Kahn glided noiselessly through the dark forest, the moon's rays piercing the leafy canopy here and there like silvery spears. As he glided, the demon sensed a section of the forest where the creatures in the trees were absent. Flapping his great wings, he moved higher and higher until he could grasp a tree branch with his long claws, their sharp tips piercing the wooden cube as if it were soft flesh. Hanging beneath the forest roof, Kahn closed his eyes and just listened to the land. He could sense his prey off in the distance. They were moving across the floor of the forest, the tiny gray-skinned one shining bright in his mind's eye like a single star on a dark sky. The magical power in that tiny gnome felt delicious. Kahn looked forward to devouring him. But then he sensed something else in the sky, on one of the islands that floated high overhead. The magic of another enchanted creature pierced the dark canopy of his mind. It was faint, barely alive, but it was there and full of magical power.

"There is muuuch to devourrr in this laaand," Kahn said in a deep, grumbling voice, his drawn out words more like a song than speech. "I will connnsume you all, but when it is timmme. Kahn has learnnned to be cautioussss and patient."

The demon smiled a wide, toothy smile that would have terrified any creature, then dug his claws deeper into the tree and watched, and listened, and waited.

CHAPTER 12

WOODCUTTER

Gameknight leaned on his shovel and worked at the thick soil before him. His iron tool strained under the effort, but it was more effective than a pick axe.

"Are you sure we need to be digging a hole?" Hunter asked, breathing hard with exertion. "We just came out of a hole and it was filled with monsters."

"I told you, if we build an underground lair, we can hide in it without anyone or anything seeing we're here," Gameknight explained. "Crafter and I did this a long time ago, when I first came into Minecraft. I remember it as if it were yesterday, but that was in my timeline, before Weaver was kidnapped and everything changed. Did that happen in your timeline?"

The young villager nodded, his blue eyes looking down into the widening pit.

"That was back when I was still an old man," Crafter said. "The creepers were after us, led by Erebus."

"Yep, and because we were underground, they didn't know where to look." Gameknight's shovel pierced through the block of dark brown soil, then started to work on a new block. "If we'd been in a house on the surface, they would have blown us to bits."

Crafter nodded.

"That was a fun story," Hunter said with a sarcastic smile.

They had dug down four blocks, and now were expanding the walls, each member of the party excavating in a different direction, while the wolves stood guard on the surface.

"Woodcutter, I don't know how you ended up in Crafter's village. In my timeline, there wasn't a Woodcutter there. How did you end up in his village?"

"Well . . . it was during the war with Herobrine," the tall NPC said.

"Your village joined with Crafter's village at the beginning of the war?" Gameknight asked.

The tall NPC shook his head.

"So you joined the fight later?"

An uneasy silence filled the dirt-lined hole. The User-that-is-not-a-user glanced around at his comrades. Many shook their heads as if subtly pleading with him to stop.

"What happened?" he asked.

"OK, I'll tell you the tale," Woodcutter began. "But I have to tell it my way, as it's too difficult to think about otherwise. So don't interrupt or ask questions until I get through it." Then the big NPC lowered his voice. "*If* I can get through it."

Woodcutter cleared his throat, then began. "There was always a competition between me and my twin brother."

"Stonecutter was his name, right?" Crafter asked.

The tall villager nodded his head almost imperceptibly.

"As I was saying, there was always this contest; who could cut the most wood versus who could cut the most stone. It wasn't just a brotherly contest with good-hearted ribbing; we were also competing for our father's respect. You see, our father was a builder, and Builder appreciated what you could build with your hands. He was deeply competitive and only respected those who were the best in their craft. So me and my twin competed for our father's respect."

"That's terrible," Gameknight said. "A father shouldn't choose between one son and the . . ."

Woodcutter raised his hand to silence him, then went back to the story.

"Since we were kids, our father heaped praise on the one that did better in school, or was faster, or stronger. He encouraged us to strive to be the best we could be, not to satisfy ourselves, but to satisfy him. For everything we did was to please him.

"The two things our father respected most were strength of body and skill with tool. He praised whichever one of us could lift the most stone or wood, or who could dig or chop the most, or build the best thing. Whomever he considered the best, Builder would include in discussions with the village elders, or take on hunting trips, or have him sit at the head of the table for dinner.

"My mother, Baker, was always the peacemaker, trying to bring me and my brother together. But as we grew older, the competition, fueled by our father's affections, became worse and worse.

"Being twins, we often argued over who was the best and who should be considered the oldest and the leader of the family, after our dad. The arguments became more heated as we grew older until finally a challenge was issued: one final contest to determine who was best. I don't remember who challenged who, but we both wanted to defeat the other and finally win the undying respect of our father. The contest was: who could build the most fantastic thing with their tools and materials, wood versus stone.

"I'd won the last couple of contests and my brother had been getting angrier and angrier as more of our father's affection slipped away, so this was his chance to regain respect again.

"We both began to cut. One of us made an elaborate statue of our mother out of wood while the other carved an elaborate stone wall complete with sweeping curves, deep spirals, and ornate images scratched into the stone face. We worked for days, foregoing sleep and food until we had put the last finishing touches on our masterpieces.

"When the contest was done, our father inspected the work. He looked at the wooden statue of our mother, examining every little detail, inspecting every nuance. He then went to the stone wall, admiring the rugged construction and artistic craftsmanship. Builder ran his fingers along the intricate pictures etched into the surface of the walls and stepped back to appreciate the magnificent curves that soared over the wall. Both creations were fantastic, but to our father, there always had to be a winner."

He paused for a moment as he relived the memory in his mind. The tall villager's face creased with sadness, a tear tumbling from one eye.

"Well . . . what happened?" Hunter asked. "Who won?"

"Our father gathered us before our house," he continued, "and made the final decision. Builder said, 'These are great works of construction and art, but there can be only one champion. Woodcutter, your statue of your mother is beautiful in every detail, but Stonecutter's elaborate wall is better.' I'll never forget what he said next. 'Stonecutter, you are truly the best. You are my true son and I am so proud of your accomplishment.' And the contest that started at birth was finally over."

"You lost," Stitcher said sympathetically. "I'm so sorry. But I'm sure your father still . . ."

"I'm not done!" he snapped, then took a slow, deep breath and continued, "You don't understand. I am Stonecutter."

Gameknight was stunned. All this time, this villager had been falsely using the name of Woodcutter, his brother?

"Why?" the User-that-is-not-a-user asked.

"Woodcutter was so distraught and emotionally devastated, he glared back at me with an expression of such complete hatred, that it made me weep on the spot." With a dirty sleeve, he wiped a tear from his cheek. "My brother stormed to the village well and sat on the ground, sobbing. But our father didn't go to his wounded son. Instead, he stayed and praised me for my magnificent creations. I was disgusted by Builder's lack of empathy for my brother, who was in pain, terrible terrible pain. I could no longer look at my father and didn't want to be his son anymore. I stormed out of the village, not knowing that was the last time I'd ever see my family.

"Later that day, Herobrine arrived at our village and destroyed it and everyone within the walls, my brother, mother, and father included."

"Woodcutter . . . or should I say Stonecutter . . . I'm sure your father and brother still loved you," Stitcher said softly. "It doesn't matter that . . . "

"You don't understand," the tall NPC said. "I wanted to win, to gain my father's respect at the expense of my brother. I was *just* as terrible as Builder. I knew my brother would never recover from losing that contest, but I tried to win anyway, just for the admiration of my father, who himself wasn't worthy of our respect. I broke my brother's heart for nothing, and will never forgive myself. Out of respect for him, I took his name, and have been trying to be the best woodcutter I could be, to honor my brother. I am no longer Stonecutter; he died at the hands of Herobrine and his monsters. I am Woodcutter, son to a wonderful mother and a spiteful father."

Gameknight was shocked. Their friend held so much grief and sorrow in his heart, it was hard to imagine how he even functioned.

"I wanted to go back to my brother, but when he'd given me that terrible, hurt, hateful look . . . it broke my heart." Woodcutter stopped to wipe the tears from his eyes. "At that moment, I knew my relationship with my brother was forever destroyed.

"I had been so sad at what I'd done to my brother that I left the village to be alone in the forest. I could have let him win. I knew he needed my father's approval more than me, but I was so competitive that I forgot about what *he* needed."

"And when Herobrine destroyed your village . . ." Gameknight began to realize.

"I wasn't even there to help with the fight," Woodcutter spat. "I was sitting in a field of sunflowers, feeling sorry for myself while my family was being destroyed. I thought I was the best son, but it turned out I was the worst."

"That's not true, Woodcut . . . I mean Stonecutter," Stitcher said. "I'm sure you're . . ."

"No, I'm not Stonecutter!" the villager snapped. "I'm Woodcutter, and will always be Woodcutter to honor my brother, the best brother and best son a father could ever ask for. I've given up the pickaxe forever and now carry this."

He held his axe in his hands, and caressed the handle as if it were his own child . . . or brother.

"I found his axe when I finally returned to the village and saw all of the devastation. There was no one left alive. But in front of the gates, I found his belongings, including his axe, surrounded by pieces of zombie flesh, skeleton bones, and spider silk. He had probably slain fifty of them before they finally took him down . . . and I wasn't there to help." He wiped a tear from his eye. "I'd do anything to have my brother and parents back," he turned and looked deep into Gameknight's eyes, "and I mean anything."

And then his voice became quiet as a whisper.

"I will never forgive myself for what I did to my brother, and not being there for them when they needed me."

"But Stone . . . ahh . . . Woodcutter, if you had been there, you'd have been destroyed as well," Crafter said.

"That doesn't matter," the grieving villager replied. "I should have been there, at my brother's side, fighting to protecting my family. Instead, I was sulking like a coward, hiding in the forest . . . I'm pathetic. Stonecutter is dead to me, forever. I am Woodcutter, the better son of Builder and Baker, and will be him until the day my HP goes to zero."

CHAPTER 13

UNDERGROUND THUNDER

They worked for the next hours in silence, Woodcutter's story having chilled them to the bone. Suddenly, the wolves patrolling the forest floor began to growl. Gameknight moved up the stone steps that led to the slowly diminishing opening in the ceiling of their hidey-hole and peered up into the woods. He couldn't see anything; darkness filled the spaces between trees, only the occasional shaft of moonlight penetrating the leafy, overhead canopy. A deep, almost imperceptible rumble moved through the surface of Minecraft, as if a hundred horses were charging straight toward them.

"Herder, quick, get the wolves in the hole," the User-that-is-not-a-user said.

Herder made a soft whistling sound and the animals instantly leapt into their hidden base and moved to his side. Gameknight then pulled out blocks of dirt and sealed the top of the hole, erasing any evidence of their presence. Once the roof was finished, and their chamber completely hidden, he pressed his ears to the earthen ceiling.

The rumbling grew louder, making not only the ceiling shake, but also the floor of their hideout.

"What do you think it is?" Digger asked.

Gameknight tried to answer, but the grumbling, booming sound grew louder as the source drew nearer. Dust fell from the ceiling, choking the air and making it difficult to breathe. The User-that-is-not-a-user moved down the steps, away from the thin layer of dirt, afraid it might fall apart at any moment. It was like being inside a thunderstorm, an underground thunderstorm.

Stitcher put her hands to her ears, trying to muffle the overwhelming sound. Tux squawked, afraid, but no one could hear her, the penguin's tiny voice too soft to be audible over the resonating cacophony.

Gameknight finally recognized the sound; it was horses, a lot of them. And the only reason horses would run in a large group like that is if it were a cavalry charge. Those horses overhead were being ridden, hard, and were chasing something. He moved next to Crafter.

"Cavalry," he whispered.

The young NPC looked at him, then mouthed, "What?"

"I said that's cavalry," the User-that-is-not-a-user said a little louder.

Crafter nodded, but his blue eyes were filled with uncertainty. "Why do you think it's horses? Maybe it's a storm or a massive thunderstorm or something else?"

But before Gameknight could respond, the horses rode away, leaving them all in a strange, almost startling silence. He turned and scanned the faces of his comrades; they all had expressions of shock and fear on their faces, just as he did.

"Do you think they're really gone?" Hunter asked quietly.

"There's only one way to find out," Gameknight said.

He pulled out his shovel and moved up the stone stairs, but before he could put tool to dirt, a small gray hand grasped his ankle. Looking down, he found Empech looking up at him, shaking his head.

"Wait! Shhhh, listen," the little gnome said, and pulled on the User-that-is-not-a-user to move away from the ceiling.

Gameknight stepped down and was about to ask Empech a question when they all heard the flapping of great wings. Then something landed on the ground overhead. The thuds of heavy footsteps pounded the dirt as something walked across the roof of their hid-ey-hole, pacing back and forth.

"I caaan sense you arrre near," a deep voice rumbled, its words slow and drawn out.

The creature walked back and forth, the ceiling overhead dropping tiny little puffs of dust with each footstep.

"Hmmm, I can feeeel you, but cannot seeee you," the creature grumbled. "You mussst have grrreat magic, grrreat magic indeed." The creature stomped back and forth one more time, scratching at the ground with what sounded like sharp claws. "Kaaahn will return, soooon."

And then the sound of huge flapping wings covered up the last of the creature's voice, beating heavily . . . and then it was gone.

"It is OK, the creature is gone, yes, yes. Empech can no longer sense it."

"What was that?" Digger asked, his face white as a ghast.

"Empech does not know," the gray gnome said, "but suspects it is true to its word, and will return."

"I don't think I like that very much," Hunter said.

"Me neither," Stitcher added.

"Flying creature or not, we must still capture Entity303 and find the portal that can take Weaver back into the past." Gameknight climbed the steps and placed the tip of his shovel on the dirt blocks. "It should be morning now. We need to get up to those floating islands somehow, and the secret must be out there somewhere in the forest. It's time we went into the sky. Everyone get your stuff."

Gameknight waited as they all put on their armor and collected their weapons and tools. Woodcutter was the first to be ready, his brother's axe held firmly in his hands, a look of determination carved into his square face. The others stepped forward, ready, but some of them lacked the look of confidence that Woodcutter portrayed. Many were shaken by the storm of horses and scared by the flying creature that had somehow sensed their presence.

Gameknight glanced at Weaver and saw an expression of anger and resentment in the boy's cold blue eyes. He knew it was meant for him, but he couldn't reveal what he knew about the boy's importance or how he would shape Minecraft with his knowledge of TNT, for it might change the decisions Weaver would make in the past . . . if they ever returned him back to his own timeline.

We must get him back to the past, Gameknight thought. *There's too much pain and regret in this timeline.*

"All of you ready?" the User-that-is-not-a-user asked.

Squawk! Tux exclaimed.

"OK . . . here we go."

Gameknight used his shovel to open the roof. He stuck his head up through the hole and surveyed their surroundings. Seeing nothing in the forest, he enlarged the hole. Once it was wide enough, they all stormed out into the slowly brightening world, not realizing that countless eyes were watching them from far overhead.

CHAPTER 14

CAVALRY

The dark sky faded as the sun rose in the east, but the strange thing was, it all seemed wrong. The sky was not turning the normal bright blue color one would expect it to. Instead, it was turning a pale, dusty green, like the color of poison.

"Are all of you seeing this sky?" Gameknight asked, just to be sure he wasn't imagining it.

"Yeah, and I don't like it," Hunter replied.

They stood in the clearing near their hidey-hole and stared up at the sky in shock.

"Look at the sun," Weaver said, pointing off to the east.

Between the branches, the sun could be seen climbing slowly up from the horizon. But instead of a bright yellow square, the sun was black, like a hole in the heavens, a smoky halo radiating from its edges.

"I think I like that even less than the sky," Digger said.

"Yeah, me too," Weaver replied.

Gameknight moved into the center of the clearing and stared up at the strange, brightening sky, the black veil of night slowly fading to the poisonous green. The others stepped forward and joined him.

Suddenly, the sound of thunder returned. Gameknight turned toward the sound. A group of horse-men were charging at them . . . zombies on horseback.

"Bows!" the User-that-is-not-a-user shouted.

Instantly arrows began streaking through the air, some bouncing off the monsters' metallic plates.

"What are those things?" Digger asked.

Squawk! Tux screeched in fear.

"They look like armored zombies," Hunter said, her bowstring humming.

"Fallen-knights, yes, yes," Empech said. "They are called fallen-knights."

"Well, I wish they'd fall off those zombie-horses," Woodcutter said with a smile.

No one laughed; they were all concentrating on their bows.

The group of decaying cavalry closed in on them, the arrows doing little to knock the zombies from their mounts.

"My arrows aren't doing any good," Stitcher exclaimed.

"Stop aiming at the armor and shoot at what's exposed," Weaver said.

"What are you talking about?" Hunter said.

Weaver moved to Hunter's side and pulled the bow from her hands.

"Oh no you didn't!" she growled.

But Weaver ignored her. Instead, he drew an arrow and fired at the zombie-horse. The arrow made the creature flash red. He fired two more projectiles at the vicious-looking animal. It disappeared with a pop, spill-ing its rider to the ground. With a smile, he handed the bow back to Hunter, then drew his iron sword.

"That's how you do it," the young boy said with a smile.

"He's right," Gameknight said. "Shoot the zom-bie-horses. Herder . . . wolves."

The lanky boy whistled, then pointed at the advanc-ing monsters. The wolves shot out into the forest, snapping at the horses' legs. Gameknight put away his bow, drew his dual swords, and charged toward the fallen knight that had tumbled from its horse. Weaver was already there, battling with the creature, his iron sword crashing against the zombie's blade.

Another fallen-knight charged at Weaver, the monster's horse snorting loud in a rage, the mount and the rider both showing eyes that glowed with a bright silvery light.

Gameknight sprinted toward the new monster, screaming at the top of his lungs. The mounted knight turned from Weaver and charged at the User-that-is-not-a-user, its iron sword held at the ready. Just as the zombie drew near, Gameknight rolled from the left side of the horse to the right. As the creature passed, he slashed at the horse and rider, his enchanted diamond blade scoring hits on both, making them flash red with damage.

Two arrows then hit the horse, taking the rest of its HP, causing it to disappear. The rider fell to the ground, hitting hard and flashing red again. Before the fallen-knight could stand, Gameknight was there, slashing at its chain mail until it fell away, exposing the creature to his deadly blades. The monster lasted only a few seconds more before it disappeared with a pop.

By now, all the horses had been destroyed, either by arrows or wolves. There were eight of the zombies left, though some of them were wounded and struggling to walk. They closed their ranks and marched toward Gameknight and his companions.

"Everyone, bows!" the User-that-is-not-a-user commanded. The villagers spread out into a wide arc as the monsters approached. "Herder, have your wolves stay back."

The boy whistled twice, bringing the wolf pack to his side.

"We don't want a battle," Gameknight said. "We come here in peace. If you hadn't charged at us with your weapons drawn, none of this would have happened."

"You are villagers," the tallest of the armored zombies said. "Our Master demands that all villagers are destroyed."

"Is that why there are the remains of a village in this clearing?" Hunter asked, a tone of accusation in her voice.

"Villagers have been outlawed for hundreds of years," the monster continued, speaking slowly as if choosing its words with care. "They would not bow to the Master and had to be destroyed."

"We're new to this land," Crafter said gently. "Your ways are unfamiliar to us. Let us talk, peacefully."

"You have been found guilty, and have been sentenced to death. Fallen-knights, ATTAC—"

"WOLVES, DESTROY!" Herder shouted before the fallen-knight could finish his statement.

The wolves leapt forward, snapping at legs and arms as they flowed past the monsters. Hunter and Stitcher opened fire, shooting their flaming arrows as fast as they could draw back their strings. Gameknight and Crafter also fired their bows while Woodcutter ran forward with his mirror-like axe cleaving through armor, Weaver at the tall villager's side. Only Digger and Empech stayed their hands, the stocky NPC hanging on to Tux, the penguin squawking and screeching.

Gameknight charged forward. He dropped his bow and drew his swords. The commander of the fallen-knights pushed past Woodcutter and kicked Weaver aside, then charged at Gameknight999. Its chain mail sparkled in the light of the black sun, magical enchantments giving the protective coating an iridescent blue glow. The monster swung at his head with an equally enchanted sword, but when the User-that-is-not-a-user blocked the attack, the zombie shoved into him. The shimmering chain mail dug into Gameknight999 as if it were covered with razor sharp spikes.

His armor has the Thorns *enchantment on it,* Gameknight realized. *Must not let him get close.*

Dropping his iron sword, Gameknight pulled out the stealeaf shield Empech had made him when they faced the Hydra in the Twilight Forest, shards of razor-sharp ice from the ice cores still protruding from the front. The fallen-knight tried to smash into him again. Raising the shield, he let the steel-blue leaves take the abuse, the glacial blue shafts from the ice cores poking into the creature's armor. He swung his diamond sword at the creature's side, slashing at the chain mail twice, scoring two hits. The monster tried to back up, but Gameknight moved forward with his adversary, the two combatants locked in a dance of death.

Pressing the shield against the monster, he slashed at the knight, hitting it again and again. The monster tried to swing his iron blade, but the shield was always there to block the attack. He hit the monster again and again. Pieces of the chain mail fell to the ground.

The zombie growled at Gameknight, its bright silvery eyes peering at him from over the shield.

"The Master will destroy you!" the fallen-knight growled. "You will not be allowed to survive. The rest of my cavalry will be here soon, and then you will be exterminated."

"We'll see."

Suddenly, a shining axe hit the monster from the side, causing the last of its armor to fall to the ground. Gameknight stepped back, hoping the monster would stop the fight, but instead, it attacked. The User-that-is-not-a-user sighed and raised his sword for the final blow, but before he could swing, Weaver was there with his iron blade. With all his strength, the young boy swung, taking the last of the creature's HP. The last of the fallen-knights disappeared with a pop, a look of despair in its terrified eyes.

"You think they really exterminated all of the villagers in this world?" Crafter asked with concern.

Gameknight glanced at Empech and raised a questioning brow.

"Empech cannot sense anyone else on the surface," the gnome said. "But I can sense things overhead, yes, yes."

"You mean on those islands up there?" Hunter asked.

The little gray pech shrugged his shoulders, then adjusted the straps of the huge pack on his back.

"Why would this Master exterminate all of the villagers in this Age?" Stitcher asked. "That kind of pointless violence is only done by a maniac."

"Or by Entity303," Gameknight added.

The young girl nodded her head, her brilliant red curls bouncing to and fro.

The User-that-is-not-a-user stared up at the floating islands and wondered what waited for them up there.

Are the Master and Entity303 the same person, or are there two villains here? Gameknight thought.

"We have to get up there, somehow," he said aloud to himself . . . but how?

CHAPTER 15

THE TRAP

Suddenly, the dull thuds of things hitting the ground echoed through the forest. It was a soft, muffled sound at first, like that of someone hitting a pillow with a baseball bat. But then the noises were punctuated with the slap of something wet hitting a hard surface.

"Over there," Crafter said, pointing to the north with his sword.

Gameknight was expecting more fallen-knights to attack, but the forest was clear of threats. The only thing he could see were the impossibly tall oak trees that extended scores of blocks into the air. After checking to make sure everyone was OK, Gameknight moved toward the sound. Herder whistled, then waved his finger in the air, making a circle over his head. The wolves spread out in a large, protective ring, watching the forest for threats.

The black sun was now far from the horizon and moving higher into the strange, green sky, but still much of the forest was cloaked in shadows; deep, dark shadows. It reminded Gameknight of the roofed forests in vanilla Minecraft, though these trees were many times taller.

As they neared, Gameknight saw the source of the noise; it was pieces of food falling from the overhead canopy and landing on the ground. Fruit, loaves of bread, pieces of steak, pork, whole cakes . . . it was a cornucopia of food falling from the leaves overhead, everything landing in a neat pile on the ground.

"There's more falling over there," Woodcutter said in wonder, pointing off to the right.

Food was falling from many trees, accumulating in little mounds. Gameknight moved closer to the pile before them and inspected the food. The apples appeared freshly picked and it looked as if steam was rising off the bread, as if it was freshly baked.

"Look, the bread is still warm," Digger said, astonished.

The other companions moved closer to examine the pile, confused glances passing from one to the next. One of the wolves barked as it moved close to a piece of steak, the other animals moving closer and licking their lips.

The smell was fantastic, almost intoxicating, like that of the cakes Gameknight's mom would bake on birthdays. He reached out to grab one of the loaves as the rest of his companions stepped closer.

"Caution is advised," Empech said suddenly. "Unexpected gifts many times come with an unexpected price."

Suddenly, a single click could be heard; it was the sound of a pressure plate being activated. Before Gameknight could react, he was jerked upward, rising high into the air; a shimmering net had wrapped itself around all of their party and was pulling them upward into the trees. Overhead, blocks of leaves disappeared, revealing an opening, the net being pulled straight through it.

"Gameknight, what did you do?" Hunter asked.

"Nothing, I just reached for the bread. I didn't even touch it."

"It seems this was a trap, and we are being taken into the trees," Crafter said.

"Thanks for clarifying that," Hunter replied.

"Be nice," Stitcher chided.

"Everyone just get ready to fight," Gameknight said softly. "I don't know what's going on, but obviously it's not good."

"Another great observation," Hunter added.

The net shot up through an opening in the leaves, then stopped after passing through the green roof, bobbing up and down. Having been in shadows for so long, their eyes were not ready for direct sunlight. They were completely blinded as the black sun beat down upon them with its bright rays. Gameknight heard the sounds of leaves being placed beneath them, the hole through which they were lifted likely being filled. He tried to look down and see who, or what was closing the hole, but their bodies were pressed too tightly in the net to move much, and the bright light made it impossible to see anything.

Suddenly, the net was released and the party fell to the leafy treetop with a thud. One of the wolves landed on Gameknight999, the creature's fur tickling his nose. Gently pushing the animal off, he stood and gazed around. A tall wooden fence surrounded the companions, effectively making a jail.

"I've had enough of this," Woodcutter grumbled.

The tall villager reached for his axe, but Gameknight placed a calming hand on his arm as he heard the creak of countless bows.

"We're trapped, but not dead," Gameknight said in a low voice. "That means they want something from us. Everyone keep your hands away from your weapons and be calm."

One of the wolves growled as shapes moved outside the fence. Herder patted the animal on its side, calming them as he spoke softly to the pack leader; likely he was getting them ready for battle.

Finally, their sight returned as eyes adjusted to the bright light of day. Around them stood twenty or thirty warriors. Archers stood atop stacks of leaves while swordsmen stood up close, ready to thrust their blades through the rails of the fence.

Gameknight looked closely at his captors. Each wore some kind of colorful mask that covered their entire face, but the bulbous nose on the mask was unmistakable; it was a villager's nose. They wore long smocks that covered them from chin to ankle, each a different color. Some had decorations sewn into the clothing, but many were ripped and torn, the adornments faded and threadbare.

Gameknight slowly reached for his sword, hoping to go unnoticed, but stopped when he heard the sound of bows creaking as arrows were drawn back, ready to be fired.

We're trapped, the User-that-is-not-a-user thought.

"You are prisoners of our great king, Iago," one of the soldiers announced.

"We aren't anyone's prisoner," Hunter growled, her bow in her hand, arrow notched.

Herder's wolves growled.

"Now let's be calm," Crafter said as he stepped forward. "I am a crafter and we are here on important business. We must meet with your king, for we believe your world is in great danger."

"Yeah, and if you ignore us, your entire world may suffer," Woodcutter said.

The tall NPC stepped forward, his axe in his hand. All of the archers turned their weapons toward him.

Gameknight smiled; he knew exactly what the villager was doing: making himself into a living shield that would stop the first volley of arrows with his body, giving his friends a chance to attack.

"Listen to me," Gameknight said, stepping up to the fence. "We must meet with your king, immediately. There is no time to . . ."

"A pech," one of the warriors exclaimed. He was wearing a faded silver mask, but the markings of gold drawn on the cheeks were chipped, the silver at the edges faded and worn. "There is a pech here. Everyone lower your weapons. It must not be harmed."

The masked villagers all lowered their weapons as Empech stepped forward, his huge backpack jingling.

"King Iago decreed ages ago that all pechs are to be brought to him, unharmed," the soldier explained. "The pech and his companions must be taken to the palace."

"Perfect," Gameknight replied. "We must speak with your king. These are dangerous times, and there is a treacherous villain in your world; King Iago must be warned."

"That's good and all," Hunter objected, "but how do we get up there?" She pointed to the floating island high overhead with her bow.

"Maybe we just jump," Woodcutter said with a mocking smile.

"Exactly," the soldier replied. "All of you, come this way."

The masked villager opened the gates and gestured for Empech to follow him. The little gnome looked up at Gameknight and nodded, then stepped forward, his pack swaying left and right with every step. Gameknight followed, glad to be out of their prison and the tense situation calmed, but he noticed the other masked villagers around them still had their weapons out. He moved to Crafter's side and spoke in a low voice.

"There is still danger here," the User-that-is-not-a-user said.

"What do you mean?" the young NPC replied. "They're taking us to their king."

"Carefully look around. They may be friendly now, but we're still their prisoners. Pass the word, quietly; we must be ready to fight."

Crafter nodded, then slowed to allow Hunter to reach his side. He whispered something in her ear, causing her eyes to narrow as she nodded, her red curls bouncing.

The soldier led them to a flattened section of the treetops. Sitting in the center was a large structure made of green-stained clay. Four columns stood on the corners of a wide platform, a huge domed roof spanning the entire structure. A wide hole was carved in the center of the dome.

Gameknight moved near the center and looked upward. Above them was a floating island. Green creatures could be seen crawling around on the underside, hanging upside down, each with a bucket. It was hard to tell from this distance, but it looked as if they were painting something on the glowing white blocks that lined the bottom of the islands.

"What are those creatures?" Crafter asked, pointing at the green creatures.

"Filthy cave-dwellers," the soldier replied, a not-too-subtle hint of disgust in his voice. "Those slaves are doing the only thing they are good for."

"And what's that?" Crafter asked.

"They paint the levitation blocks with fuel to keep the islands afloat."

"But don't some of them fall?" Stitcher asked, shocked.

"So what?" the soldier replied. "If they fall, we capture more cave-dwellers in our nets . . . just like we caught you."

"There's no excuse for slavery of any kind," Stitcher growled, her grip tightening on her bow. "I know a lot about slavery, and there is a better way."

She started reaching for an arrow, but Empech put a hand on her arm.

"We are with friends, child," Empech said in his high-pitched, almost child-like voice. "The king will answer all our questions, yes, yes."

She growled, but relaxed.

"Everyone follow me," the soldier said. He moved up to a glowing block covered with cracks, each jagged line glowing bright orange. When he stepped on the block, the soldier was instantly propelled upward, soaring into the air and through a hole in the floating island high overhead.

"That looked easy," Woodcutter said.

With his axe held at the ready, he stepped onto the block, then was launched upward just like the soldier.

"Everyone, grab a wolf," Gameknight said. "We aren't leaving them here."

He bent down and picked up the pack leader, the animal glaring at him for a moment, then relaxing when Herder patted the animal on the side. "We do this fast. Everyone stay close together. Ready?"

They nodded, wolves in their arms. Gameknight stepped onto the glowing block and shot into the air, toward the sky island, and undoubtedly his enemy, Entity303.

CHAPTER 16

PATIENCE

Kahn sat on the treetop with his wings wrapped about him, their dark leathery surfaces covering his bright red skin and making him look like a shadow on the leafy canopy. He watched as the villagers flew up into the sky islands, the small gray one going last. The magic from that tiny gnome made the demon growl with hunger.

"Yourrr magic willll be a fantassstic addition to what I'vvve taken from allll the other magical creaturesss across Minnnecraft," the red monster growled to himself.

As he watched the last of them shoot up into the air, Kahn closed his eyes and listened to Minecraft. He could feel the villagers and his gray prize on the island high overhead. Numerous mundane creatures, none of them with any magic, surrounded the villagers. When the time came for Kahn to collect his prey, the inhabitants of the sky island would pose no threat. The thought of those puny little masked creatures trying to put up some kind of pathetic defense was humorous. The demon laughed a deep, guttural laugh that sounded more like a growl.

"I cannnnot wait untilll I feassst," he muttered to himself.

With his magically-enhanced senses, he probed the island and its massive palace. He could feel all of the creatures climbing underneath the island, a few falling every now and then to their doom. Within the island, there were countless tunnels and caves where the citizens lived, some holding large numbers of soldiers.

Suddenly, Kahn sensed something . . . another beacon of magic in this mundane world. There was a source of magic on the largest of sky islands, hidden in some kind of dungeon. But this second creature did not shine as bright as the gray-skinned one. The imprisoned one was weak . . . near death. And near the dying enchanted creature, he sensed something shocking. It was something he thought he would never feel again since the destruction of his people and his world. It was one of his own kind, a young demon that also stood near the precipice of death. The revelation was stunning. Kahn thought he'd never see another of his own kind, and now there was one within reach, housed in the same dungeon with the magical creature under the sparkling palace.

"I willll free you soooon, my friend, but firrrst I must waaait to seeee what these villagers dooo," he growled, his words drawn together like a grumbling song. "When I knnnow what is happening up there innnn the skyyy, then I willl strike and devourrr all that luscioussss magic. And then my kinnn will be freed frommm their dunnngeon as I devvvour their magical neighborrr."

Extending his razor sharp claws, Kahn carved a hole out of the top of the tree, then scrunched down into the recession and sat, his black wings hiding his presence. Glaring up at the sky island and all the delicious magic up there, the great demon patiently waited.

CHAPTER 17

THE BARGAIN

King Iago led Entity303 through the palace, showing off columns of diamond blocks and statues made of emeralds. Everything was constructed to show off the incredible wealth Iago possessed. One room was even lined with gold, the very chairs and tables made of the shining metal.

A gold room . . . with gold chairs? Entity303 thought. *How ridiculous. What kind of fool needs all this gold to feel good about themselves? . . . Only an insecure child.*

The user complemented the king, pretending he was impressed with all of the obscene, gaudy displays of wealth and power, but it only made Entity303 see what a pathetically weak leader Iago really was.

They moved to the edge of the massive sky island. It was the largest in the sky by far and was another symbol of his power, and insecurity. Walking along on either side were the king's black-robed guards. Their white masks were each decorated with different types of colorful swirls, the occasional gemstone sewn into their long black smocks. Each held an enchanted gold sword that seemed to go along with the décor of the place. Entity303 knew his infused sword could easily cleave through their weapons and rend their HP from their cloaked bodies. Their puffed-up chests and bravado made him chuckle.

At the edge of the island was another catapult block, as he'd used down in the trees to get up into the sky islands. Watching the guards out of the corner of his eye, he removed his Alpha Yeti chest plate and donned his sparkling Elytra wings.

"Your Elytra are enchanted?" Iago asked.

Entity303 nodded. "I added a mending spell to them, just to keep them in tip top shape."

"That was a good idea," the king replied.

"Of course." Entity303 grinned at him. The smile was like that of a snake grinning at a mouse. It made Iago cringe a little.

The king put on his own wings, then stepped on the catapult block. He was instantly shot into the air, his long purple smock flapping in the wind, the many-colored jewels sparkling with rainbow hues.

Entity303 stepped onto the glowing block and was thrust up into the air. He waited until he was at his highest, then opened his wings and glided on the gentle east-to-west breeze. Below him, King Iago glanced about looking for the user. Entity303 laughed . . . what a fool the king was, only thinking in two dimensions and forgetting about above and below. In the distance, he could see hundreds of floating islands sprinkled across the sky, some larger than others. A few of them had a column of black liquid shooting up into the air: oil. NPCs moved about around the oil, collecting it into buckets, then pouring it into mechanisms to refine it into fuel. Most of the fuel was used to keep the levitation blocks operating beneath the sky islands, keeping them in the air. This was the heart of Iago's power over the other people in this world.

A stream of black-cloaked guards flew up from the sky island, each of them like dark shadows in the sky. Their white masks made them almost seem like bodiless apparitions haunting the sky, but the gold sword in each of their dark hands reminded Entity303 of what they truly were . . . threats. Eventually, Iago would have his guards turn on him at the last instant and try to double-cross him. But the fool had no idea who he was dealing with. The idiotic king thought Entity303 was just after power within these digital worlds. He had no idea what his real plan was . . . the destruction of everything in Minecraft. If Iago knew the truth, he probably would throw everything he had at the user to stop him. But fortunately, the ruler did not know what was at stake. And besides, Entity303 knew he could count on one thing with Iago . . . his greed.

They glided to the next island. It was not as large as Iago's primary domain, but still fairly big. A cluster of trees sat on one edge, the dark trunks reaching high into the air, but the leaves on the trees were silver instead of green, the individual leaves reflecting the sunlight like tiny little mirrors. They sparkled as the breeze caused the leafy blocks to sway to and fro.

Entity303 landed amongst the silverleaf trees, far enough away from Iago and his guard so they could not attack him the instant he landed. Thick red grass covered this island, just as it covered all the others; it was a natural feature of this world, and the grass tended to grow everywhere, as long as it was not dug up. Once disturbed, it would not grow back. With his hand on the hilt of his deadly sword, the user approached the king. The guards were looking in all directions, but when they spotted him, the dark warriors lined up in front of their king.

"There you are, my friend," Iago said in a jovial tone.

Entity303 was certain there was an insincere smile under his exquisite mask.

"Show me your part of the bargain," the user said without hesitation, unwilling to exchange the false pleasantries. "I don't have time for pretending we're friends when we aren't. Forget about your games and let's get down to business."

"Of course," the king replied, his tone now cold and lethal. "We both see the reality in things. It is not important that we're friends. It is only important that we both profit from our exchange."

"Exactly," Entity303 added. "Now show me what you've done since I've been gone."

"Very well."

Iago turned away from the user and walked toward the cobblestone building. The sunlight sparkled off the gold stitching and jewels that adorned his purple smock. It was spectacular to behold, and distracting; Entity303 knew that was why the king did it . . . to keep his adversaries off balance ever so slightly.

A set of iron doors marked the entrance to a huge structure, but no button or lever was visible. He knew his diamond pickaxe would go through the cobblestone easily enough, but he stayed his hand and watched the ruler.

Reaching up with a black-gloved hand, the king pressed a stone button that was hidden on the cobblestone wall. Pistons and mechanisms actuated and moved underground, causing a set of cobblestone blocks to slide into the ground, creating an opening in the wall. Iago smiled at his cleverness and walked through the opening. The black-clad guards waited, their gold swords shining in the light of the shadowy sun.

Entity303 smiled at their pathetic attempt to intimidate him with their butter-swords. He enjoyed knowing all of them would soon be gone when he completed his plans and destroyed Minecraft forever.

Stepping to the opening, Entity303 walked through. Inside the cobblestone building, he saw a partial construction of a rocket; only the engines and nose cone were missing. The body of the craft stretched up to the ceiling, where there was a gigantic hole in the stone roof, allowing it to lift off when completed.

"Why isn't it finished, as per our agreement?" Entity303 asked.

"We wanted to finish refining the oil into rocket fuel for you. But when we started building the rocket for you, as per the designs you left us, we found the plans for the engines were missing. So that slowed the construction and fueling for a while."

"Why are you surprised, Iago?" Entity303 said. "You aren't a fool. You know that's my bargaining chip. I told you that I'd supply you with designs for rocket engines for all of your islands if you built me a rocket and filled it with fuel and oxygen generation equipment. If I gave you the engine schematics, then you'd never have built anything."

"First of all, it is *King* Iago," the monarch corrected. "And secondly, I thought we had an agreement that was based on trust."

"Trust . . . ha! You don't know the meaning of the word. The only reason you're king is because you control most of the oil fields. And that oil is made into fuel and painted over the levitation blocks by your slaves, to keep your islands floating in the sky. Once you have rocket engines on all your islands, you won't need the cave-dwellers anymore and those with their own oil will have to kneel to you and beg for rockets to keep their islands in the air. You'll have complete control over everyone, but only after you have the design for these engines."

"You see the situation perfectly," the king said.

"None of your subjects trust you, and you trust none of them. Your whole society operates on a system of bribes and threats." Entity303 moved to a window in the structure and looked out at the trees that sat far below. "The tree-dwellers are the lowest of the low in your society. That's what happens to people who run out of money or disobey you. They're sentenced to forever work the nets in shame. I know that's where you send your enemies and competitors. As soon as they were seen as a threat, you stole their wealth and sentenced them to the trees. Let me ask you, how many of those wretched souls did you once call friends?"

"Friendship is just a convenience and not really that important," Iago said. "Besides, I only sent people to the trees if they deserved it." A wry chuckle trickled out from behind the king's golden mask.

"And by the numbers down there in the trees," Entity303 continued, "I'd say you were threatened by a lot of them."

"Well . . . after I destroyed twenty or thirty families and stole their fortunes, the other citizens seemed to have no problems with my being their king."

"So you eliminated all the threats?"

"There are always threats," Iago growled. "I would make an example of a wealthy family every now and then. Plant some evidence showing they were traitors or criminals, and then sentence them to the trees. A couple of demonstrations showing what happens when you disobey always gets the sheep in line, so to speak."

Entity303 stepped away from the window. He felt the urge to remove his wings and put his chest plate back on, but he knew if he had to flee, or was thrown off the island, the Elytra wings were the only thing that would save his life. Anyone falling without Elytra . . . was doomed.

The cave-dwellers who displeased the king, or didn't work hard enough, or were just unlucky enough to be noticed, were frequently thrown off the sky island just as an example to the others. In fact, the king had a special platform of sand made just for the occasion. Entity303 found it a bit barbaric, but he did see the effectiveness of a good, lethal example to keep the peasants and slaves in line.

"Maybe in a day or two, we'll be done with the fueling process and finished with the nose cone, then we can complete our trade," Iago said.

"This had better be ready or I'll be forced to take matters into my own hands." The user drew his sword, the weapon glowing with an angry yellow light. "The one thing I'm good at is destruction, and I won't hesitate to destroy everyone on your puny islands to get what I need."

The guards in black stepped forward, the eyes behind their white masks glowing with anger.

Entity303 looked at them and laughed, then turned and faced Iago. "Get this completed, or else."

He then put away his sword and walked through the collection of guards and left the building. As he passed the king, Entity303 thought he saw a look of fear behind the eye holes of the King's golden mask. It made the evil user laugh again as he leapt off the island and flew through the air.

CHAPTER 18

MEETING WITH THE KING

They were all shocked at the opulence and grandeur of the room in which they waited for the king. The floor was a complex mosaic of polished stone, granite, and diorite, the geometric designs incredible to behold. The walls were made of quartz, with the same mosaic from the floor sweeping up into the walls. Tall columns of pillar-quartz stretched from the floor to the ceiling high overhead, holding up a massive domed roof made of stained-glass. Splashes of color filled the room as sunlight pierced through the multihued ceiling. Every shade and tint imaginable was present in the roof overhead, and as a result was projected down on the floor. It was awe-inspiring and took Gameknight's breath away.

At the far end of the room sat the king's throne. It was made of solid gold, with blocks of diamond, lapis, and emerald decorating the sides. It sat atop a gentle pyramid of quartz, raised four blocks above the floor. The throne gave Gameknight an uneasy feeling; he'd seen one like that long ago, but he couldn't remember where.

Higher up, a balcony ringed the room. It stuck out a few blocks from the wall, with dark, shadowy alcoves recessed into the back of the terrace. Likely these alcoves were passages that would allow visitors to gain access to the raised platform.

The size and height and elaborate decorations in the room made Gameknight and his friends feel insignificantly small; likely that was their purpose.

"You remember those creatures we saw working beneath the sky islands?" Hunter asked in a low voice. "I think they were the same as those monsters in the caves. I remember some of them clinging to the ceiling of the tunnel when we escaped their caves."

"It isn't right that they enslave those creatures," Stitcher growled. "Slavery is wrong, no matter the reason."

"Couldn't they leave if they wanted to?" Weaver asked.

Stitcher flashed the boy an angry scowl that made him take a step back, as if she were about to strike him.

"You don't understand," the young girl explained. "I was a slave in Malacoda's fortress in the Nether for what seemed like an eternity. The constant state of fear and terror just makes you want to give up and wish for . . . you know."

"Did you ever give up?" Woodcutter asked.

"No, I knew my sister would fight through an army of blazes and ghasts to save me. I just had to keep my spirits up and wait for my opportunity. When the army of villagers came into the Nether to fight Malacoda and his monster horde, the slaves revolted and fought back. You see, for the first time, the slaves had one thing they didn't have before."

"Weapons?" Crafter asked.

She shook her head.

"Armor?" Weaver asked.

"No, it was simpler than that," the young girl said. "For the first time, we had hope, and that's more powerful than the sharpest blade or the stoutest shield.

"We used our shovels and pickaxes and bare hands. Most of the guards had been pulled away to delay the villagers while Malacoda finished his portal to the Source. That was when we saw our chance. We attacked the wretched wither skeletons, then fell on the blazes before they knew what was happening.

"More than half of the slaves were destroyed, but we didn't care. That feeling of hope made us realize we weren't really alive as slaves, and taking this chance to fight was better than going back to work and staying a slave again. When we finally destroyed all the guards, Malacoda had already fled with his army and we found all of you there." She paused for a moment. "Freedom never tasted so sweet." Her voice then became soft, like a whisper, but cold and hard like a jagged piece of glass. "We cannot leave those creatures enslaved. I cannot allow it and I'll do whatever is necessary to free them."

"Stitcher, I understand what you're saying, but I'm not sure if we can really help them. Beside, we must remember that we're following . . ."

"All hail King Iago," an announcer yelled from the corner of the room.

Just then, a lavishly clothed individual entered the room from the opposite side. He wore the most spectacular purple robe, gems and elegant stitching sparkling in the torchlight, a gold mask over his head and face. Light reflected from the shiny covering, casting spots of light all across the throne room's walls and floors.

"Welcome, friends," a voice boomed from the other end of the hall. "Welcome to the sky islands."

Gameknight stepped forward. Instantly, a group of black clad soldiers, each carrying an enchanted gold sword, stepped forward. Every one wore a white mask, with delicate designs painted on the cheeks and sides. No two were decorated the same save for the bulbous nose that hung right beneath the eye sockets.

The wolves growled. Holding up a hand, the User-that-is-not-a-user signaled for Herder to keep control of the animals.

"King Iago, we are visitors to your world on an important mission," Gameknight explained. "There is reason to believe you and all your citizens are in great danger."

"Great danger!" Iago laughed. "I doubt that. But please, before you tell me more, it would be rude to continue without proper introductions. As you know, I am King Iago, absolute ruler of these lands. Who do I have the pleasure of meeting?"

The User-that-is-not-a-user was a little shocked by this formality. Entity303 was somewhere up here in the clouds, and that meant they were all in danger. He didn't have time for this nonsense.

"Well?" the king asked.

Gameknight sighed.

"Very well, I am Gameknight999. Behind me is Crafter, the oldest NPC in Minecraft."

"He looks but a child," the king chuckled.

"Crafter has more years of experience than anyone in this room," Gameknight said.

He noticed Iago shift his gaze toward Crafter; his eyes glowed faintly silver for just an instant, then faded back to darkness behind his golden mask.

"These two are Hunter and Stitcher, the greatest archers in Minecraft," Gameknight said, gesturing to the sisters. "Behind them are Digger and Woodcutter, the greatest craftsmen in Minecraft. On the other side are Herder, the animal whisperer, and my friend Weaver." Gameknight pointed to the boys. "And last but not least, Empech."

Squawk! Tux exclaimed.

"Oh, and of course our penguin-friend, Tux," Gameknight added.

Iago stood from his throne and slowly approached, the black-robed guards moving with him. He clasped his gloved hands behind his back and looked them over from head to foot as if he were inspecting a cow about to be purchased.

Gameknight's gaze was suddenly attracted to the smallest movement on the balcony. Someone was hiding in a dark alcove. He glanced at Hunter, then tilted his head subtly to the balcony. She moved only her eyes and peered into the darkness, then slowly nodded her head. Stitcher saw the move and glanced to the balcony as well.

"So the rumors are true, you really have a pech with you," Iago said as he came to Empech. "This is fantastic."

"Why is it so incredible?" Crafter asked.

"Well . . . ah . . . we haven't had a pech in these lands for . . . um . . . a hundred years," Iago explained. "They are magical creatures of great power. It has been law of the land that if any are found, they are to be kept safe and brought to the king."

"You haven't seen a pech for a hundred years, but you have a law about what to do if one is found?" Weaver asked. "Really?"

"Hush now, child," Iago said, "the grown-ups are talking."

Weaver tensed. The wolves growled.

"We have a great respect for pechs and want to make sure they are safe in our lands," the king said. "This is a great day. We'll need to have a celebration. Where is my assistant, Othello?"

"Here, your Highness," a voice said at the back of the chamber.

A short NPC stepped out of a doorway. He wore a silver and white robe with small crystals of lapis stitched into the garment. His mask was colored emerald green, with spirals of white and yellow meticulously painted on the sides.

"Othello, organize a banquet tonight to welcome our new friends and of course the most honored of visitors, a Third . . . Empech," Iago commanded.

"A Third?" Gameknight asked, but was ignored.

"Yes sire, it will be done," Othello replied, then quickly fled back into the passage, his booted feet pounding the floor as he scurried off.

Iago turned and walked back to his throne. He moved gracefully up the steps, his purple robe flowing about him like a colorful wave, then turned and sat on the raised golden chair and gazed down at them.

"So what brings you here to our peaceful community?"

"We are here pursuing a user like myself," Gameknight explained. "His name is Entity303 and he's a very dangerous individual. We have reason to believe he's plotting something that will lead to the destruction of this world, if not all the worlds of Minecraft."

"The destruction of Minecraft . . . oh my," Iago replied, but with complete insincerity in his voice.

"The fallen-knights on the surface said villagers were outlawed," Hunter said. "Is that true?"

"Yeah," Stitcher added. "Is it?"

The king laughed. "Fallen-knights . . . please, they are nothing more than bandits trying to take advantage of you. They cannot be trusted, for they are the lowest creatures in our society, save for the cave-dwellers, of course. Do not pay any attention to those knights, they are *fallen* for a reason."

"You mentioned cave-dwellers," Stitcher continued. "Are those the creatures climbing around under your sky islands?"

"Of course," King Iago replied. "They have a critical job, tending to the levitation blocks. Without their hard work, all of our islands would fall to the ground."

"Why is it just cave-dwellers are doing the work and not any of your villagers?" Hunter asked.

"You're new here and obviously do not understand," the king said. "The Mogs and Glugs have claws that allow them to hold on while they coat the blocks with fuel. No one else could do that. And besides, they are only cave-dwellers, and are expendable. Many more of those beasts exist in the caves. They make the perfect labor force."

"You mean *slave* labor force," Stitcher clarified.

"Of course," Iago replied, stating it as if it were some kind of obvious, universal truth.

The young girl growled with rage. Gameknight put a hand on her shoulder, trying to calm her before things got out of control.

"King Iago, we have journeyed far to come here," Crafter said. "Perhaps there is someplace we could rest before your magnificent banquet begins."

"How could I have been so insensitive," the ruler exclaimed. "Yes of course. Othello, where are you . . . fool!"

"Here, sire," the assistant said as he stepped out of a dark passage.

"Show our visitors to the guest quarters," the king commanded. "Take a couple of servants with you in case they need any help." He gestured to the black-clad guards.

"Yes sire, it will be done."

Othello walked across the hall, then gestured for Gameknight and his companions to follow. He led them into a side passage, followed by two of the black-clad guards.

"I'll take you to the finest quarters," the servant said. "The elaborate decorations and wealth displayed in these rooms will show what high regard our king holds for all of you."

"We appreciate it," Crafter replied.

They moved into passages that led downward into the dark recesses of the sky island. For some reason, Gameknight didn't believe they were being taken to guest quarters. He suspected everything Iago had just told them was a lie and they were in terrible danger.

CHAPTER 19

PRISONERS

"Othello, heading so far down under the palace seems like a strange place to keep guest quarters," Crafter said. "Are you sure you're taking us to where your king intended?"

"I'm sure of it," the masked NPC replied. "Only the most special guests are brought down here. Few know of these quarters, but the king only wants the best for you and your friends."

Crafter glanced worriedly at Gameknight999, a suspicious look on his square face.

Glancing over his shoulder, the User-that-is-not-a-user checked to see if the two guards were still with them. They were walking behind the last of the wolves, their enchanted swords always held at the ready. Suddenly, Empech stopped in his tracks, his blue, gem-like eyes wide with shock. He let out a loud high-pitched screech that echoed through the passage.

"Empech, what is it?" Stitcher said, rushing to his side.

"Another . . . another," the little gnome mumbled, alarmed. "I sense another."

Just then, a similar, high-pitched cry floated through the tunnel.

"That was coming from up ahead," Gameknight said. "It sounded as if someone was in pain." He drew his diamond sword. "Come on!"

He pushed past Othello and charged down the passage, the rest of the company following.

"Herder, protect the rear," Gameknight shouted without looking back.

He heard a whistle, then the growls of wolves as the furry animals blocked the two guards from following.

"This is bad, this is bad," stammered Othello. "The king must be notified."

Footsteps echoed through the corridor as the masked assistant ran back to Iago.

Ahead, Gameknight found a side passage blocked with an iron door. Next to the door were a series of levers; it was a combination lock on the door.

"Anyone have an idea how to figure out the combination?" Gameknight asked.

Another scream came from the behind the door. This time it was weaker.

"I do," Digger said.

The stocky NPC set Tux on the ground and stood before the door.

"Well?" Hunter asked. "How do you figure out the combination?"

"Like this," the stocky NPC said. He pulled out his pickaxe and smashed the door again and again until it shattered. "All you have to do is knock."

"Nice," she replied, then dashed through the opening, into a dark passageway.

"You can't go in there," one of the dark-robed guards feebly protested.

The two warriors charged forward. A wall of fur and fangs blocked them from advancing. One of them made the mistake of hitting one of the wolves.

"ATTACK!" Herder shouted.

The wolves fell on the two guards. Their gold swords swung this way and that, trying to hit the wolves, but the animals were too fast for them. Just then, an arrow streaked through the air and hit one of the soldiers. Another shaft followed the first, hitting its target, causing the guard to disappear with a pop. The second soldier, seeing his comrade fall, dropped his sword and ran.

"Let him go," the User-that-is-not-a-user said. "We need to see what's happening in here."

Herder whistled, recalling his wolves.

"Gameknight, you need to get in here," Hunter shouted from within the passage. "All of you, get in here."

"Herder, stand guard while we investigate," Gameknight said. "Weaver, Woodcutter, and Hunter, stay here and make sure we have a way to escape if needed."

Not waiting for a response, he dashed into the passage, Crafter, Digger, and Empech following close behind.

The tunnel plunged downward, going deeper into the bowels of the floating sky island. The passage was dark, but a flickering light filled a chamber at the end. When they reached the bottom of the stairway and entered the room, Gameknight found himself in a dungeon. The walls and floors were made of mossy cobblestone, with chests of weapons and armor along the walls. Against the far wall were two cells, the back walls, floor and ceiling made of obsidian to discourage any attempts to tunnel in and out. The front of the cells were covered with iron bars, likely to allow easy access for the king to come down and gloat.

In the left cell was a tiny demon-like creature with red skin and tiny black wings. It had a pair of pointy white teeth that stuck up on either side of its mouth, a similar white pair of stubby horns growing from the top of the creature's head. Its feminine-looking bright orange eyes darted about from one NPC to the next, clearly unsure what was happening.

"Empech, what is this creature?" Gameknight asked.

"A fire-imp, yes, yes," the gnome answered.

"I am Deimos, a fire-imp of the Cassio clan," the fire imp said.

Empech was about to say something when a creature in the right cell stood and approached the bars, stopping the gnome before he could start.

"Hmmm . . . another," the deep voice said. It was weak and near death. "Forpech never thought it would see another."

Empech rushed to the bars and held out a hand. Inside the cell was another pech, like him. The imprisoned creature had the same diminutive size and protruding jaw. But instead of blue, gem-like eyes, this one had black, seemingly bottomless eyes that were filled with sadness and pain.

"Digger, you think you can figure out the combinations to these cells, too?" Gameknight asked.

The stocky NPC smiled, something he rarely did, then smashed through the bars on the pech's cell. As soon as there was an opening, Empech reached for a splash potion of healing and threw it on the creature, drawing him back from the edge of death.

"What about the other one?" Crafter asked.

"Release the fire-imp," Empech said as he helped his fellow pech out of the prison cell. "She is a friend, yes, yes. All fire-imps are friends."

Gameknight nodded. Digger smashed the bars until they shattered. The fire-imp tried to walk out of the cell, but it too was dangerously close to death.

"Empech, any more healing potions?" Crafter asked.

The pech turned toward the fire-imp, then threw a potion of healing with such speed that it was almost impossible to see as it streaked through the air. When it hit the little creature, red sparks surrounded the little red monster as its health was replaced. A second splash potion hit the creature, rejuvenating the last of the creature's HP.

Deimos stood a little taller, though she was still shorter than an NPC child.

"Who are you?" Empech asked his newfound cousin.

"I am Forpech, and have been imprisoned by Iago for many many years," the dark-eyed gnome said, his voice deep, like distant thunder. "That mad king . . . hmmm . . . seeks to rule all the creatures of this land. If they do not kneel before him, then . . . hmmm . . . they are destroyed. That is what happened to the fire-imps. Hmmm . . . they once were plentiful, but when Iago destroyed the blood grass on which they fed, the fire-imps perished."

Gameknight glanced at Deimos. He could see the creature's orange eyes, rimmed with yellow, glowing bright with hatred as she relived the atrocity in her mind.

"We have company coming," Hunter shouted into the passage. "You might want to speed up whatever you're doing and get up here so we can figure out how to escape."

"Right, let's get back with the others," Crafter said.

"Wait," Forpech grumbled.

The gnome, gray-skinned like Empech, moved to one of the chests that lined the walls. He opened the wooden box. The hinges screeched rusty complaints of neglect, but yielded to the creature's stubby three-fingered hands. Reaching into the chest, Forpech withdrew a large back-pack that seemed to be made of the same brown cloth as Empech's pack. Putting his arms through the straps, Forpech donned the gigantic pack and adjusted the weight until it sat correctly on his tiny frame. Reaching back into the chest, he withdrew what looked like a small wand, the tip holding a forest-green gem.

"Hmmm . . . Forpech is now ready," the gnome said.

Howls of alarm echoed through the passage.

"The wolves," Crafter said.

"They're coming," Digger added, a look of fear on his face.

"Come on, let's go," Gameknight said.

They charged back up the dark stairway they had descended to reach the dungeon. At the top, Gameknight found Weaver and Woodcutter building defenses in the passage as Herder yelled out commands to wolves that were nowhere to be seen.

"Lots of swords coming through the passage," Hunter said. "I don't think we're getting out that way."

"Forpech, is there another way out of the dungeons?" Gameknight asked.

"Hmmm . . . Forpech has been here a long time, let me think."

"How 'bout you think faster?" Hunter said. "We don't have much time here."

"Hunter, be nice," Stitcher said, punching her sister lightly in the shoulder.

"Owww," she replied with a smile.

"If memory serves, Forpech was brought in from the other direction," the pech said, his low voice reverberating off the walls.

"I remember being brought in that way as well," Deimos said, her voice crackling and snapping like the sound of a small campfire.

Hunter turned, not having noticed the fire-imp until then, and was shocked at what she saw. Instinctively, she drew an arrow and aimed at the little red creature. Stitcher reached out and pushed her bow down to the ground.

"This is a friend," Stitcher said. "And remember what the rule is . . . we don't shoot our friends."

"But it's a . . ."

"I am a fire-imp and my name is Deimos," the creature said. "I have been a prisoner of King Iago for longer than I can remember. Our common enemy bonds us together."

"You hate Iago too?" Hunter asked.

Deimos nodded her tiny demon-like head.

"Then you're all right by me," she replied.

"Herder, recall the wolves," Gameknight commanded. "It's time to get out of here."

The skinny boy whistled, the shrill sound echoing off the stone walls. Instantly, the wolves, some of them limping, returned. When they had passed by the defenses built by Woodcutter and Weaver, they sealed in the wall, hopefully to slow Iago and his troops for a while.

"Come on, let's try to get out of here," Crafter said.

The young NPC turned and sprinted down the passage, the pechs and the rest of the party following. Gameknight waited for the last of the wolves to pass, then followed behind. As he ran, he could feel the ground shake. The sound of a hundred boots pounding the floor of the passage filled the air. Whatever Iago's response, it would involve a lot of soldiers, and that was a problem—a big problem.

CHAPTER 20

SACRIFICE

They ran through the dark passages, Gameknight using the Moonworm Queen to light the way. Not wanting to show Iago and his forces where they went, the User-that-is-not-a-user had Woodcutter stay at the rear. The tall NPC smashed the glowing moonworms with his shining axe as he passed, extinguishing their yellow light. They hoped it would make it difficult for their pursuers to follow.

Forpech seemed to know where they were going, turning at junctions and choosing side passages when he felt they were correct. The User-that-is-not-a-user asked how he knew where he was going, but the tiny gnome only mumbled something unintelligible in his deep voice and continued on.

They found a set of stairs that led upward . . . that seemed like a good thing. The stairs continued upward for a bit, then leveled off and opened into a massive chamber of stone, the ceiling twenty blocks high and barely visible in the darkness. Tall columns of cobblestone were spaced throughout the room as if holding up an impossibly heavy ceiling. Gameknight knew this was only cosmetic; the rules of Minecraft physics did not require anything to hold up the ceiling, as long as it was not made of gravel or sand.

Multiple passages pierced the side of the vaulted chamber, each one dark and foreboding. But then the sounds of boots began to echo from one of the tunnels, the flickering of a distant torch casting an orange glow on the walls.

"They're coming," Digger said, his voice shaking.

Squawk, added Tux.

Woodcutter ran to the glowing passage and placed blocks of cobblestone over the exit.

"That will at least slow them down a little," the tall NPC said,

He moved back to Gameknight's side, the fluorescent yellow-green glow of the Moonworm Queen making Woodcutter's red smock look orange in the strange light.

"Hmmm . . . this way, the surface is this way," Forpech said, his low voice sounding like the grinding of massive stones.

"I can smell fresh air," Empech said, his screechy words echoing off the walls and pillars. "The surface must be near, yes, yes."

They turned and ran, Gameknight placing more of the moonworms on the ground while Woodcutter stayed at the back, breaking them with his axe as he passed. Echoes of boots floated to them through the air, with the flickering of more torches filling the passages.

"There's more of them," Stitcher said in alarm.

"I know, I can hear them," Gameknight replied. "We just need to hurry."

"Where is it we're actually running *to*?" Hunter asked.

"I'm working on that," the User-that-is-not-a-user replied.

Suddenly, the sound of footsteps filled the hall and torches could be seen in the distance bobbing about as the soldiers ran through the chamber. In the flickering light, the golden mask of Iago could be seen sparkling in the distance.

"They're right behind us," Crafter said, his voice cracking with tension.

"I know, I know," Gameknight said. "Faster . . . everyone run faster."

"That's your plan?" Hunter asked.

The User-that-is-not-a-user's reply was more speed. He sprinted as fast as his legs could move him, the others keeping pace and staying together.

"An exit ahead," Forpech growled. "Hmmm . . . we will be out of this chamber soon."

"Good," Hunter replied.

Gameknight glanced over his shoulder and saw more of the king's soldiers pouring into the huge room, the side passages filling with torches and glistening swords.

Ahead, the gigantic room narrowed down to a single corridor, just a single block wide, with torches lining the wall. Gameknight put away the Moonworm Queen and drew his bow. Aiming upward to maximize the range, he fired an arrow, the shaft instantly bursting into flame as it leapt off his enchanted bow. The burning projectile arced through the air, then struck some poor soul thirty blocks away. A scream echoed off the walls.

"Quickly, everyone follow Forpech through the passage," Gameknight said as he shot another arrow. "Herder, send some wolves with him, to make sure the pechs are kept safe."

The lanky boy knelt and whispered to the pack leader, then stood and drew his sword. Half of the pack darted forward while the other half waited for the rest of the party to enter the narrow tunnel. The pounding of the approaching feet grew louder as the rest of the companions bolted into the passage. After the wolves followed the last of them, only Woodcutter and Gameknight remained.

"I can slow them down here for a while," Woodcutter said. "It'll give you time to escape."

"NO! We leave no one behind. I lost Herder once and will never forgive myself for that. I lost Weaver and look where we are now. I'm not losing anyone else."

"Very well. Then let's go," the tall NPC said. "Run, I'll follow."

Gameknight nodded, then turned and sprinted into the cave, Woodcutter right behind. Glancing at the ceiling, the User-that-is-not-a-user saw patches of sandstone amidst the stone. Likely there was sand up there as well. Woodcutter looked up as well, then gave Gameknight a wry grin.

"Let's get going," the tall NPC said.

Gameknight nodded and took off running. He heard a smashing sound as he ran. Glancing over his shoulder, he saw Woodcutter breaking the torches on the wall.

"No sense in making it easy for them to follow us through this tunnel," the towering villager said with a smile. "Keep going, I'll break these torches and be right behind you."

"OK," Gameknight replied.

He sprinted forward, slowly catching up with the others. The sound of Woodcutter breaking the torches slowly grew softer; he couldn't run as fast as Gameknight while still extinguishing the burning sticks.

Eventually, the User-that-is-not-a-user caught up with the rest of the party. The wolves growled at his approach, but when they saw him, their fur slackened and their eyes faded from red to black.

"Where's Woodcutter?" Stitcher asked.

"He putting out the torches behind us," the User-that-is-not-a-user replied. "He'll be here in just a minute."

Suddenly, there was a rumbling sound, as if part of the ceiling had collapsed for some reason. A great billowing cloud of dust filled the passage, making many of them cough.

"The tunnel is collapsing!" Weaver shouted.

"Quickly, we need to get out of here," Stitcher added.

Suddenly, the clash of metal on metal could barely be heard through the collapsed passage; it was the sound of battle.

"Woodcutter!" Gameknight moaned. "He's trapped back there."

A loud battle cry filled the passage.

"WOODCUTTER!"

The tall villager's shout echoed off the walls and seemed to make the very fabric of Minecraft quake in fear. At first, they had all thought the NPC's battle cry was for himself. But now, they all knew it was for his long lost brother, whose forgiveness he'd never receive, but that he'd also never stop trying to earn.

More of the passage collapsed as the sound of battle grew more intense. Now shouts of pain and fear percolated through the tunnel. Gameknight could imagine the tall NPC's axe cleaving through the approaching soldiers, none of them able to get past and attack from behind. It was the perfect place to slow the army, that is . . . until his HP finally gave out. The NPC wouldn't be able to hold them back forever.

"We have to go help him," Weaver said. "We can't just leave him there."

"The passage is likely filled with sand and gravel," Crafter said. "We'd never be able to dig through in time."

"If everyone goes back down this tunnel, hmmm . . . then everyone perishes," Forpech, his deep voice adding gravity to his words. "We must honor the sacrifice being given and flee."

"But it's Woodcutter," Stitcher moaned.

Gameknight looked at her and saw the sorrow in her eyes, but also saw the realization of what must be done.

She sighed.

"We must continue," the young girl said with resignation. "For Woodcutter!"

Turning, she continued through the passage, away from the sound of battle.

"My sister is right," Hunter added. "FOR WOODCUTTER!"

Her red curls flowed through the air like a crimson wave as she spun around and followed Stitcher. The pechs continued, followed by the fire-imp and Crafter.

The wolves growled at the sound of battle. They wanted to attack and stand next to their companion, but Herder would not let them. Instead, he whistled, then followed the others through the passage.

With Tux under his arm, Digger shoved Weaver forward and started running.

SQUAWK, SQUAWK, Tux shouted to their companion. Gameknight thought he saw a tear fall from the little animal's eye.

Finally, Gameknight was alone. The sound of fighting raged, slowly growing louder as Woodcutter backed up gradually, giving ground to avoid a sword or arrow. Gameknight desperately wanted to go help his friend, but knew he couldn't. Minecraft needed him to finish this thing with Entity303 and return Weaver to the past. Woodcutter was doing what he had to do, to help his friends and hopefully put the timeline back in order. That was how he had chosen to honor his brother, by saving all of his friends with his brother's axe.

Raising his hand in to the air, fingers spread, Gameknight gave the salute for the dead to his friend, who had not perished yet, but would soon.

"WOODCUTTER!" he shouted, then added, "STONECUTTERRRR!"

He clenched his fist with all his strength, every bit of anger and rage and sadness being crushed into his palm. When his knuckles began to pop, he released his hand and lowered it to his side. Turning, Gameknight followed his friends, leaving Woodcutter to his fate.

"I make this promise to you, Woodcutter," the User-that-is-not-a-user said aloud as he ran. "Your sacrifice will not be in vain."

The sounds of battle grew quieter as he moved farther away, but the clash of metal on metal was still easy to hear. Then suddenly, the sounds of battle stopped and were followed by a great cheer.

Woodcutter was no more.

And as he chased his friends, Gameknight999 wept.

CHAPTER 21

OFF THE PRECIPICE

Gameknight's legs burned, but he continued to sprint until he caught up with the others. By the time he reached them, his tears had stopped, and all he felt inside was emptiness, as if some part of himself were now missing.

"Woodcutter?" Hunter asked.

The User-that-is-not-a-user shook his head and looked at the ground.

"I'm gonna make that Iago suffer," Hunter growled as they ran.

Ahead, the end of the passage seemed to brighten. One of the wolves howled in delight.

"That's the exit," Herder said, "We finally made it out of those tunnels."

"Not all of us," grumbled Weaver.

Gameknight cast him a glance, but he'd already sped forward, toward the outlet.

They shot out of the passage and onto a field of bright red grass, trees with silver leaves swaying in the breeze. A light brown footpath stretched out in front of them, two blocks wide. The pechs and wolves stayed on the dirt walkway, running as fast as they could from the dungeons they'd just escaped.

Clouds choked the sky. Huge rectangles masked the stars overhead, leaving just the smallest of openings for the moonlight to shine down upon the land. It made the silverleaf trees sparkle as if they were enchanted, but then the magic evaporated as the clouds covered the moon and plunged the land into darkness.

Suddenly, twenty archers on either side stepped forward, bows drawn and ready. But for some reason, they didn't fire.

"Keep running," Gameknight shouted.

He pulled out his shield and held it in his left hand, his shimmering diamond sword in his right, the enchantments casting a purple glow about the group.

They ran down a sloping hill only to find sheer stone walls lining the walkway. Raised wooden seats extended up on the other side of the wall, as if the pathway were leading to some kind of amphitheater.

And then, the path ended at the edge of the sky island. Everyone skidded to a stop and turned to look back along the path. Archers stood along the edge of the path, clearly waiting for something. Gameknight turned to the right and ran along the edge of the island, looking for an escape route. After going maybe twenty blocks, he encountered tall barricades with more masked soldiers standing atop the battlements. None of the warriors fired their arrows, but would likely attack if any of them tried to scale the wall.

Turning around, Gameknight ran back along the left side of the sky island. As before, he encountered a wall of brick that stood eight blocks high, more masked warriors staring down at them. They were trapped.

"Everyone, back to the main path," the User-that-is-not-a-user said.

The party moved back to the dirt path, then clustered near the edge of the floating island. Just then, an army of soldiers emerged from the shadowy passage and approached along the path. Each warrior was clothed in flamboyant colors, their masks and smocks sparkling with gems and shining gold and silver stitching. At the front were Iago's black-clad guards, the golden-masked ruler walking a few paces behind. Archers now filled in the bleachers on either side of the pathway, each with bows notched and arrows drawn back.

Gameknight knew they were trapped, and had no place else to run. Slowly, he turned and faced the line of shadowy soldiers, his shield held at the ready.

"Everyone, stay behind me," the User-that-is-not-a-use whispered. "Herder, keep your wolves back. We don't want to do anything to cause those archers to shoot."

His comrades all moved backward onto a large section of sand that sat at the edge of the sky island, torches lining the perimeter, splashing a flickering glow on the companions. Gameknight backed up as well until he too was on the sand.

Suddenly, all grew dark as a large group of clouds floated overhead, blocking out all light from the moon and stars overhead. Warriors lit torches and held them aloft, casting circles of light on the observers.

Iago pushed through the crowd of soldiers and stood at the head of his army. He held in his hands a shining axe, its blade glistening, polished to mirror perfection; it was Woodcutter's.

"My friends, it seems we have gotten off on the wrong foot," Iago said, his words slow, deliberate, and threatening. "You have some things that belong to me; they are my trophies. If you do not return them to me, I will be most upset."

"You had a pech imprisoned," Gameknight accused. "And you destroyed the entire race of fire-imps."

Deimos stepped forward and stood at Gameknight's side.

"Those little creatures were no threat to you, yet you eradicated them anyway," Stitcher said.

Squawk, added Tux.

"You're a genocidal monster; you're no friend of ours," Crafter said, his sword in his hand, eyes filled with rage.

"Yes, the last fire-imp. She was a special treasure," the ruler said. "We went to great effort to exterminate all of her species across the land. We found all they could eat was the red grass . . . so we dug it all up. They quickly starved, but I saved one just to remember the joy of destroying them."

"They didn't do anything to you," Gameknight said, enraged. "They didn't deserve to be destroyed."

"Those fire-imps were of no use to me or my plans for ruling this entire world." Iago took another step forward and glared at Gameknight999. "Anything that does not help me is eliminated."

"Like the cave-dwellers you enslave?" Crafter asked.

"Oh yes, the Mogs and Glugs are very important. They keep the levitation blocks covered with fuel so our islands stay floating high above everything else. We must be above everything else in this land because we are better than everything else down on the ground or in the trees."

"Living on the ground, in villages like normal NPCs, wasn't enough?" Hunter asked.

Iago smiled mockingly.

"Of course not," the king replied. "Everything and everyone must look up to me as I rule them, and keeping the sky islands afloat is paramount to this. But now, after completing negotiations with my new friend, Entity303, we will have rocket engines keeping my islands afloat. We have no need for the cave-dwellers."

"So I suppose they'll be destroyed as well?" Digger asked, an angry scowl on his square face.

"Of course. If they are no use to me, they will be discarded like so much garbage." The king looked down at Woodcutter's axe, then smiled cruelly and threw it off the island. "There's the last bit of garbage from your friend. One less malcontent to deal with."

They waited a full minute as the axe fell the impossibly long distance to the forest floor. Finally, it was heard striking the ground, and shattering into a million pieces.

A look of sadness spread across Gameknight's face as the last piece of Woodcutter was erased from Minecraft. The wolves growled.

"That belonged to our friend, Woodcutter," the User-that-is-not-a-user hissed. "He was the best of us, with more courage or honor than you'll ever have."

"Ha . . . courage, you know nothing about it," the king said. "He was nothing. In fact, he wasn't courageous at all. That villager begged on his hands and knees for mercy. I let him weep like a baby for a while, and then I destroyed him myself."

"You're a liar," Hunter snapped. "Woodcutter would never have begged for anything from you."

"You know so little, girl," Iago said. The other soldiers saw their king laughing, and did the same. As soon as Iago stopped chuckling they all became silent, doing exactly what was expected. "Your tall friend saw me in all my glory and just put down his axe and begged for his life at my feet, like the coward he was."

"How many of your soldiers did you sacrifice to finally get past Woodcutter?" Gameknight asked. "Twenty . . . thirty?"

Many of the soldiers shook ever so slightly in fear at the talk about Woodcutter; likely he'd taken many of them down before his HP dropped to zero.

Just then, Entity303 stepped out from the crowd and glared at Gameknight999.

"So the coward emerges from behind the king's shadow," Gameknight said.

"I'm done toying with you, Gameknight999. My plans are proceeding perfectly. I see you have my little villager friend with you." The user stared straight at Weaver. "I'll spare your life, villager, if you come with me now."

Entity303 held out a hand to Weaver, a wry smile on his square face.

"You'll have to destroy me before you ever lay a hand on my friend Weaver." Gameknight said as he put away the shield and drew his iron blade, the two swords held ready for battle. He moved in front of the young boy. "You want him . . . come and get him!"

Just then, Herder whistled and pointed to Weaver. The wolves formed a tight circle around the boy, their eyes burning a bright red.

"We protect our friends," Gameknight said. "But that's something you wouldn't understand, because you have none."

Entity303 tensed at this comment; Gameknight smiled.

"I remember where I've heard the name Entity303 before now. I've heard the rumors about you, the programmer who went a little crazy. In fact you were too crazy for Minecraft, weren't you? So they fired you." Gameknight glared at Entity303. "You're a lonely, pathetic programmer who was fired from Minecraft. And now you skulk around in the shadows, trying to get back at them by messing with their game, instead of facing them directly."

Entity303's face turned a dark shade of red as his eyes narrowed, an angry glare directed at his enemy.

"You're alone, friendless, and pathetic," Gameknight said, pointing at his adversary with his diamond blade. "I pity you."

"I'm tired of this," Entity303 said to the king. "Destroy them now, and I'll throw in some extra rocket engine parts."

Iago smiled. "Deal."

The king moved to a button that sat on a gold block nearby, a line of dark redstone powder leading away from the shining cube and disappearing underground. He smiled at Gameknight999 and glanced at the sandy ground on which the companions stood, then pressed the button. The redstone ignited, glowing bright, the crimson signal causing pistons to move somewhere beneath the ground.

Suddenly, the blocks under foot simply fell away, the torches lining the sandy platform instantly quenched. The companions, pechs, wolves, and fire-imp dropped from the sky island and plummeted into the open air.

Every nerve in Gameknight felt as if it were aflame as terror filled his soul.

We're falling to our deaths! his mind screamed at him. *What have I done to my friends?*

As they dropped, Gameknight saw Entity303 peering over the edge of the sky island. He locked eyes with the vile user and felt consumed with hopelessness and despair as the evil programmer laughed at the sight of their destruction.

CHAPTER 22

CAVE-DWELLERS

The world around him was moving in terrifying slow motion.

Gameknight glanced at his friends, the horrified expressions on their square faces telling the tale . . . this was the end.

Tux fell alongside him. He knew the penguin could flap her wings and float down gracefully, but the animal clearly would rather be with her friends than fly away.

I hope you start to fly just before we hit, Gameknight thought.

He locked eyes with Crafter just before the moment when he thought they'd fatally smash into the trees.

Any second now, he thought. *Here it comes . . .*

A sound like leaves being chopped apart filled the air. Gameknight tried to process the sound, but fear now ruled his mind.

Another moment passed, somehow . . . and . . .

SPLASH!!!

The impossible happened. They somehow landed in a freezing cold pool of water.

We're alive, we're alive!

"WE'RE ALIVE!" Gameknight shouted.

He pulled out a torch and held it high over his head. The yellow glow illuminated the pool, showing his friends standing in knee-high water, a rocky floor underfoot. Far overhead, a gigantic hole looked like it had been carved into the rocky ceiling directly under the edge of the floating island, the leaves in the treetops somehow cut away as well. Cave-dwellers gripped the stone ceiling, each holding cubes of tree leaves.

"That hole up there doesn't look like an accident," Crafter said, thinking out loud. "It's right under the platform where Iago drops his victims."

"You see those green cave-dwellers," Stitcher said, pointing to the opening. "I heard them breaking the leaves as we fell."

Gameknight nodded glanced upward. *That's what I heard, too.*

The cave-dwellers were now replacing the tree leaves back across the opening. They carefully sealed the opening, then clung to the ceiling, ready to tear at the leaves if needed.

"Won't Iago be surprised to see us again," Hunter growled as she drew her shimmering bow from her inventory. It cast a sparkling purple glow around them.

"Hmmm . . . best to put weapons away," Forpech said in his deep voice.

"Empech agrees, yes, yes. We are not alone."

They all turned and stared into the darkness that wrapped around the shallow pool. Far away, long vines hung down from a rocky face, the berries on the vine glowing white. They were torch berries, but were too far away to add any illumination.

Unexpectedly, tiny points of red light emerged from the dark veil that wrapped around the company. They grew more numerous, as if they were getting closer. Gameknight stared at them, trying to figure out what these things could be, their numbers growing and growing until . . . one pair blinked.

Digger pulled out a torch and held it high over his head. Nearby was a rough-hewn stone wall. The User-that-is-not-a-user quickly pulled out the Moonworm Queen and fired the glowing insects on the wall. The squiggling things stuck and instantly cast a fluorescent yellow glow. All around them stood the green creatures they'd first encountered, the ones that had chased them from the caves when they had entered into this world: the cave-dwellers.

Hunter reached instantly for an arrow, but Forpech's gray hand settled on the girl's arm, calming her.

"Friends, I believe . . ." the gnome started to say, his deep voice sounding like distant thunder. "Hmmm . . . we have nothing to fear."

A pair of the largest monsters stepped forward. They were both huge, muscular creatures, with thick, strong arms, and short, stout legs. Large white tusks stuck out from the creatures' mouths, their tips razor sharp. One, the male, wore brown shorts, and was completely bald. His two pointed teeth shone bright in the yellow light, one of them cracked and chipped at the end. The other, a female, wore a dark brown dress and a tan shirt. She had light brown hair, almost strawberry-blond, with a neat part down the middle. Her eyes were warm, more orange than the red of her companion. The two creatures looked down at Gameknight. Their eyes did not seem angry or vicious; rather, they looked sympathetic and kind.

Deimos stepped forward, wading through the water, then climbed up onto the stone floor and stood next to the pair. As the tiny demon approached, the female crouched and held out a hand to the tiny red monster.

"We have not seen a fire-imp for a long long time," the female said in a grumbling, growling voice that sounded terrifying at first, but the kindness in her eyes made any fear instantly evaporate. "Where have you been, little red one?"

"The king captured me," Deimos said, smoke floating out of her mouth. "He wanted to have the last fire-imp as a trophy to remind him of the destruction of my kind."

"You are safe now; all are safe in our caves," she said, looking down at Gameknight999 and smiling. "My name is Thea and I am a Glug. This is my husband, Thorin. He is a Mog. We are the cave-dwellers, enemies, and often slaves, to King Iago."

Thea held a welcoming hand out to Gameknight999. "Come out of the water before you freeze."

Gameknight glanced at Hunter. She shook her head, unsure what was happening. But then Gameknight looked down at Forpech. The grizzled old gnome had a huge smile on his wrinkled gray face, his dark eyes glowing with hope. He nodded his oversize head.

Reaching out, the User-that-is-not-a-user took Thea's hand and moved out of the water. As he stepped aside, Forpech and Empech came forward, their huge packs soaked and dripping wet. When the Mogs and Glugs saw the two pechs, they instantly went to one knee and bowed their heads.

"Thirds . . . thirds . . . thirds . . ." they chanted almost reverently.

The sound of more cave-dweller voices emanated from the darkness around them.

"Hmmm . . . please stand, there is much to do," Forpech said. "Iago will soon launch an attack on the cave-dwellers. He no longer . . . hmmm . . . needs you to service the levitation blocks."

"Yes, yes, he will likely try to exterminate you as he did to the fire-imps," Empech added.

Digger then waded forward. He scooped up Tux from the water and placed her on the ground next to Deimos, then patted the little fire-imp on the back.

"We aren't gonna let that happen, are we?" The stocky NPC turned and looked at his companions, then stared up at Gameknight999. For the first time in a long time, an expression of courage blossomed within Digger's green eyes.

"I guess we aren't," the User-that-is-not-a-user replied.

"But how can we fight back against the fallen-knights?" Thorin asked. "We have no weapons and have no way to make any."

Digger glanced around at the stone walls of the massive cave world. Gameknight saw where he was looking, and instantly the puzzle pieces began to tumble around in his head.

"Yes, we'll use stone, and there is ample wood outside," the User-that-is-not-a-user mumbled to himself.

"What?" Hunter asked, confused.

"Shhh . . . he's figuring it out," Crafter said.

"But how do we get up there?" Gameknight whispered, his mind going through all the possibilities. "Of course, the nets. But there will be many soldiers up there, how can we . . ."

Just then, Hunter placed a torch on the ground, illuminating the dark cave. Stitcher placed another to the right while Herder placed one to the left. Each torch pushed back the darkness and revealed a green body for each set of eyes that glowed in the darkness. There were hundreds of Mogs and Glugs all throughout the caves.

Gameknight looked at the sea of green faces, then turned and faced his companions, a huge smile on his face.

"You figured it out?" Crafter asked.

Gameknight nodded, then turned and look up at the tall Mog and Glug. "We aren't gonna let Iago eradicate the Mogs and Glugs." He glanced at his friends and gave them a smile. "We must get back up to the sky islands and find someone who's very important to all of us. While we're there, we might as well destroy Iago's army and free the cave-dwellers."

The Mogs and Glugs grunted and growled, their excitement growing.

"I have a plan," the User-that-is-not-a-user contin-ued "but it will be incredibly dangerous."

"Will it be more dangerous than just standing around and waiting to be exterminated?" Thorin asked.

"Probably not," Gameknight replied, "but still dangerous."

The Mog turned and glared into the darkness. Suddenly the cave became alive with more red spots staring back at them. A grumbling sound began to fill the air, like a storm of gigantic bumble bees, but then added on top was a *thump, thump, thump.* Hunter went farther in the cave and placed more torches on the ground and walls, illuminating the caverns with flicker-ing yellow light. Mogs and Glugs by the hundreds—no, thousands—were moving closer, all of them making a growling sort of noise in their throats as they pounded their fists on their chest.

Thorin made the same grumbling noise. It was a guttural sort of sound that came from deep down inside the creature. He pounded on his chest along with the rhythm, then held his fist up high. Instantly, the cave grew silent, with all eyes fixed to him and his Glug wife, Thea.

The pair turned and looked down at Gameknight999, their muscular frames and towering bodies suddenly intimidating. Here was the army that could overthrow Iago and restore peace to these lands, if only they would be willing to stand up and fight.

"You have the Thirds," Thea growled, her voice like a deep rumbling earthquake, "and you have the fire-imp. We have no doubt you are creatures of honor." She moved forward and stood directly in front of Gameknight999. If she were going to strike him down, there was nothing anyone could do about it. "I say it is time for the cave-dwellers to no longer be afraid of the forest. I say it is time for the Mogs and Glugs to no lon-ger starve in the darkness." Her voice grew louder. "I say that our brothers and sisters will no longer be slaves for the sky-dwellers." The pounding of chests began again like the rhythmical beating of a ceremonial drum. "We have cowered in the darkness too long. Now it is time to fight!"

The cave erupted in a storm of growling thunder as the Mogs and Glugs pounded their chests with heavy green fists. Gameknight looked up at Thea and smiled.

"Iago has no idea what's about to hit him," Crafter said at his friend's side.

"Nor does Entity303," Gameknight added. He turned to Digger. "It's time we got to work."

"I couldn't agree more," the stocky NPC said as he pulled out his pickaxe and started to dig.

CHAPTER 23

KING IAGO

"**W**hat do you mean the cave-dwellers are gathering in the forest?" the king asked. "That's *my* forest!"

"Yes, sire," Othello said. His emerald green mask shook with fear.

"Are they taking the food and getting caught in my nets?" Iago asked. "They would be much easier to destroy if we had them ensnared."

"Well . . . your highness . . . it's, ahh . . ."

"What is it, Othello? Spit it out!"

"Well, they're avoiding the nets, as if they've figured out what they do," Othello explained. "They're staying away from the food and everything."

"Very well, if they want to make this difficult on themselves, then so be it."

The king turned and faced one of his black-clad guards. Their white mask was adorned with jagged lightning bolts painted in gold, with small rubies glued at the end of each crooked line.

"Commander, perhaps we need the fallen-knights," Iago boomed. "Those pathetic villagers are now gone. There is no one to help the cave-dwellers. We will swoop down upon them like a plague and destroy them, as we did the fire-imps."

"Yes, sire," the commander replied.

"I recommend caution," Entity303 said from the shadows.

The king turned and glared at the user with annoyance, his eyes glowing with the shining silvery hue.

"Gameknight999 has a way of showing up unexpectedly," the user added.

"You mean the user that I just threw off my island, and watched as he fell to his death?" Iago laughed. "I destroyed him in exchange for more rocket engine parts. He is gone . . . forever."

"Prove to me he's destroyed, then. If you can't, you had better be careful. That user has a way of causing trouble wherever he goes."

"Ha! You're afraid of ghosts," the king mocked. "I'm not concerned about any of those users . . . they're gone."

"As you wish," Entity303 said.

He stepped toward King Iago. Instantly, the guards moved closer to their ruler, gold swords held at the ready.

These idiotic creatures. I could easily destroy them all if I wanted. He gave the soldiers a wry smile, then stepped back.

"What of our bargain? Are you ready for me to deliver the rocket engines?"

Entity303 reached into his inventory and placed one on the ground. The engine grew to full size as soon as he released it. Iago looked at the motor with a rabid hunger in his eyes.

"Are you ready to complete our trade?" the user asked again.

"Ahh . . . well . . . we're still transferring the refined fuel from the oil fields to the palace," Iago said.

He pointed at a nearby window. A cluster of islands was visible in the distance. Tall black columns of liquid spewed into the air, spraying the ground and workers that toiled nearby; Entity303 knew it was oil. He also knew Iago had those islands well-guarded; the oil was the source of Iago's wealth, and the root of his power over the rest of the sky-dwellers. Without the oil, all their lands would crash to the ground.

Entity303 picked up the engine with one hand and drew his blazing yellow sword with the other. The motor instantly shrunk when he lifted it off the ground. With a smile, he put the mechanism back into his inventory.

"You had better hurry up and honor our agreement, or I'll go find my own oil," Entity303 growled. "I allow you to rule these lands because I need you. But if that situation changes, then *everything* will change."

"Your threats do not interest me, *user.*" Iago spat the word from his mouth as if it were poison. "I am the King here, and everyone takes orders from me. Now, be gone. I will summon you when I am ready. But right now, I have a species of cave-dwellers that needs to be driven to extinction." Iago turned to the guard commander. "Assemble the fallen-knights. Send them into the caves and have them destroy everything!"

"Yes, sire."

The warrior turned and walked to a small group and began issuing orders. In seconds, the black-clad soldiers sped away, each having been given a specific task that would hasten the destruction of the cave-dwellers on the forest floor.

Moving to the window, Entity303 watched as soldiers leapt from the sky island, then snapped their Elytra wings open mid-fall and glided through the air, all of them heading down toward the forest floor.

Entity303 watched the messengers descend, then turned and glared at Iago.

"You try my patience," the user growled. "I will not wait forever. When I return, be prepared to finish our bargain. This is your final warning—next time, I will just *take* what I need."

Before the King could reply, Entity303 stormed from the chamber, his glowing sword thirsting for destruction.

CHAPTER 24

FALLEN-KNIGHTS

The ground began to shake. Thunder was coming, though it wasn't the thunder of a storm . . . it was the thunder of war.

In the distance, a group of galloping horsemen slowly emerged from the haze. At first, they were only faint apparitions, like ghosts from some terrible nightmare. But slowly, they changed to dark silhouettes, only the silvery eyes of the horses and riders visible. As they drew closer, razor sharp swords and sparkling chain mail came into view.

The black sun slowly began to rise, casting warm shades of red and orange across the landscape, the long shadows of the impossibly tall trees giving the ground a striped look. When the light fell upon the Mogs and Glugs, the horses reared and galloped straight at them.

Quickly, the green monsters started placing blocks on the ground to offer some protection. They left space between the columns of stone through which to fight. The cave-dwellers held their empty fists into the air, growling and shouting at the oncoming assailants. The fallen-knights in return held up their glistening iron weapons and laughed, expecting this to be an easy battle. The horsemen charged straight at the green creatures and urged their mounts to gallop faster, the violent riders anxious to destroy.

The sun rose higher, allowing the warm hues of sunrise to fade, replaced by the poison-green of the morning sky.

The fallen knights were now only a dozen blocks away. The Mogs and Glugs began a grumbling sound deep in their throats, then pounded their chests slowly, rhythmically, as if beating out a cadence. As their enemy came closer, they beat their chests faster.

The mounted monsters were now only eight blocks away. Their swords sparkled in the morning light. They slapped the backs of the horses with the flat of their blades, urging them to run swifter. The Mogs beat their chests faster, but now also pounded on the ground with their black-clawed feet. At the same time, the Glugs reached into their inventories with both hands.

When the armored zombies were only three blocks away, the cave-dwellers stopped making any noise and stood perfectly still. The lead knight slowed his mount, unsure what was happening.

Suddenly, the ground on either side of the horsemen erupted as stone shovels cut through the dirt, allowing cave-dwellers to leap out of the holes they'd hidden in. At the same time, the Glugs near the battle line pulled their hands out of their inventory. They each tossed a stone sword to the nearby Mogs, then drew blades for themselves.

Suddenly, what had looked like certain victory for the fallen-knights now became the exact opposite. The cave-dwellers, armed with stone swords, attacked. At the same time, more of the green monsters poured out of the nearby passages, each brandishing their newly made weapons.

Gameknight stepped out of his hole and dove into battle. His two swords were a whirlwind of destruction as he moved from zombie to zombie. He slashed at the zombie horses, tearing HP from their decaying bodies, then slashed at the zombies' chain mail. Flaming arrows streaked down upon the monsters, Hunter and Stitcher firing from archer towers the Glugs had quickly constructed as part of the plan. Wolves darted throughout the battle, not standing in one place, but rather streaking through the chaos, biting and snapping at zombie legs as they passed.

And then suddenly, Weaver was at Gameknight's side, his iron sword slashing at an armored zombie. Moving *with* each other, their attacks were like a synchronized dance; one blocked while the other struck. They fought like the good old days, during the Great Zombie Invasion, each watching the other's back. It was as if all had been forgiven between the two of them.

Some of the zombies, now without their mounts and limping from injury, broke from the battle and tried to run away.

"Herder, stop those knights from escaping," Gameknight shouted.

Herder whistled and pointed. His wolves instantly responded. A wave of fangs and fur descended upon the fleeing monsters. A group of Mogs ran with the animals, their strong legs able to keep pace with the wolves. They caught the zombies and fell upon them like a terrible storm. The fallen-knights tried to defend themselves against the stone swords, but were then attacked by the wolves. When they turned to face the wolves, the cave-dwellers tore at them with their blades. The escaping creatures lasted only moments, then were gone.

Gameknight climbed one of the piles of stone placed by the Glugs and pounded his swords against his diamond chest plate. It was the signal for the Mogs and Glugs to cease fighting and step back. The huge green creatures moved away from the few surviving fallen-knights, but continued to growl at them.

"Give up and your lives will be spared," Gameknight said, his loud voice ringing with confidence.

"Surrender . . . to cave-dwellers?" one of the zombies said. "That would make us lower than them. There is nothing lower in society than cave-dwellers."

"You don't get it," Stitcher snapped. "Life isn't about your position in society or about how much power you have or how much wealth, it's about friends. Life is about helping someone you don't even know, just because you can. Life is about learning how to be the best person you can be. It's not about vying for power or influence. That's only for the short sighted or the foolish." She put away her bow and stepped forward, moving close to the knight that had spoken. Removing her diamond helmet, she looked directly into the eyes of the soldier. "It's time to put away your swords and build instead of destroy."

"Well," the soldier said. He lowered his sword and took a step closer to the girl, his eyes still glowing with the silvery light. "Maybe you are right."

He moved another step forward, then suddenly raised his sword and swung it at Stitcher's head. Everyone gasped. No one was close enough to stop the attack.

Suddenly, a blast of light flashed through the air and hit the soldier in the chest. His body was enveloped in a cocoon of rainbow light that shifted from one color to the next in such rapid succession it was hypnotizing.

Gameknight turned and watched Forpech step forward, his wand held out in front of him. The green orb at the tip glowed bright as it bathed the fallen-knight with magical power. But unlike Empech's magical weapon, Forpech's did not seem to cause any pain to the wielder or the victim. It only made their eyes open wide, as if they had just understood something incredibly important, like some kind of universal truth.

Some of the surviving armored zombies took a step toward their comrade. Forpech flicked his wrist, causing the stream of colorful magic to move from one to the next, hitting and enveloping each for just an instant. After each were struck, the monsters let go of their swords, then dropped to their knees and wept.

Gameknight was stunned. He ran to Stitcher's side and eyed the zombie commander with caution. The creature no longer held his sword; it had been cast aside. Looking down at himself in disgust, he stripped off his armor and threw it to the ground as if it were poisoned. Tearing his helmet off, the zombie looked up at Stitcher, the silver light gone from his eyes. He bowed his head, begging for forgiveness.

"The Third has taught me a great lesson I will carry forever," the zombie said. "I can only hope you will forgive me, little sister."

Tears streamed from the zombie's eyes as he looked up at Stitcher, compassion and grief covering his scarred face.

The young girl stepped forward and put her hand on the creature's shoulder, then caressed the back of his bald head.

"We all must work together, to make the world we live in a better place for everyone," she said gently.

The zombie nodded his head, then turned and looked at the other surviving fallen-knights. They nodded as well.

Gameknight smiled, then turned and looked at Forpech, a million questions in his head. He started to speak when the gnome raised a hand.

"Time for questions later," the little gnome said in his deep voice. "Hmmm . . . Forpech thinks another plan is needed."

He pointed to the silvery nets with a three-fingered hand.

Gameknight turned and saw the nets slowly being raised up into the trees, the piles of food—the bait—just left on the ground.

"Apparently, the path to the trees no longer exists, yes, yes," Empech added.

"That seems like a problem, Gameknight," Hunter said. "You have any ideas?"

"Well, we could . . ." the User-that-is-not-a-user started to say, but was interrupted.

"He nears. I can feel him . . . HE NEARS!" Deimos shouted, making small smoke rings puff from her nose.

"What?" Gameknight asked.

He turned and gazed down at the little fire-imp, hoping she would explain. But all Deimos could do was stare up into the air, a look of surprise and awe on her little red face. She pointed up with a clawed hand, as if reaching for something in a dream. Gameknight turned and looked up. A flash of red shot past his vision, too fast to see what it was. But then, a heavy thump resounded just behind him, the ground shaking as if struck by a meteor.

Slowly, he turned, his gaze passing across his friends. They all had looks of shock and fear etched across their square faces. Hunter's mouth hung open as Crafter struggled to say something, but could not find the words.

Spinning around, Gameknight found a gigantic, bright red demon standing before him, its leathery black wings extended, sharp black claws at the ends. The monster stared at Gameknight999, its bright orange eyes blazing with magic. It raised a muscular arm and pointed at the User-that-is-not-a-user.

"I ammm Kahn, annnd I havvve come to feasssst," the monster growled, his voice like thunder. "You arrrre in mmmmy wayyy."

The creature was huge, taller than any monster Gameknight had ever seen before, except for maybe the Hydra. Two razor sharp tusks stuck up from its mouth, the white teeth nearly as large as Gameknight's sword. The red monster's body rippled with muscles as it glared at the villagers, its gaze finally settling on Empech and Forpech, the demon's eyes filled with ravenous hunger and a thirst for violence.

CHAPTER 25

CONFRONTATION WITH KAHN

The huge demon flicked his wings, knocking a few leaves off that clung to the ends. They made a slapping sort of sound when fully extended, causing everyone to jump just a little. The monster drew them in a bit, and it looked like he was getting ready to strike.

The Mogs and Glugs grumbled in fear, many of them running back into the safety of their underground tunnels. Others knelt before the monster, ready to surrender to save their lives. But Thea and Thorin held their ground, unwilling to go from one tyrant to another without a fight. Gameknight glanced at the pair and saw them standing tall, but he also noticed both trembling ever so slightly, as were his companions; everyone was terrified, especially Gameknight999.

"I commme for the smmmall onessss," Kahn said, pointing at Empech and Forpech. "Whennn I have devvvoured their mmmagic, then I willll take your enchanted weaponssss."

"Not likely," Hunter growled. She notched an arrow to her bow and pointed it at the demon. "You'll have to destroy me first. Others have tried, and all have failed."

Kahn laughed a loud booming laugh that was part chuckle and part deep guttural growl; it was terrifying.

"You won't be harming any of my friends," Gameknight said, trying to sound brave even though he could hear his voice shaking. "I will not allow it!"

"Annnd who arrrre you?" Kahn said, his long words stringing together into a continuous growling sound.

"I am Gameknight999, the User-that-is-not-a-user and defender of Minecraft," he said, marshaling every bit of courage he had. "We're about to stop the genocide that Iago seeks to perpetrate against the Mogs and Glugs. I won't let you hurt any of my friends, and I'll do everything in my power to stop you." He turned and glanced at Weaver, then stared again at the tall demon. "There is nothing more important to me than my friends, and they're all standing behind me. I won't let you hurt any of them, not while I still draw breath."

Gameknight took a step forward. He tried to hold his body still, but the tremors of fear were too much to control. "I don't have time to be distracted by you, so if you mean to fight, then bring it on. But I'd rather we were allies, than enemies."

The tall demon moved closer and stretched out its wide, black wings again. Shining talons extended from each of the creature's fingers and toes, the pale horns protruding from his head gleaming in the morning light.

Gameknight swallowed nervously. This was a dangerous creature, strong and lethal. It could likely pick him up and fly high into the air, then just drop him. He gripped his swords firmly, but refused to yield; his friends needed him.

Just then, Weaver stepped forward and stood at his side, his iron sword in his small hands, shaking. Herder moved to Gameknight's other side, the wolf pack leader beside him and growling angrily. The lanky boy reached down and patted the lead wolf on the side, stilling the growls, the entire time keeping his eyes fixed upon Kahn.

Gameknight glanced at Herder first, then looked at Weaver. He saw anger glowing in Weaver's blue eyes, but it was not just focused on the tall demon. Weaver glared at Herder with jealousy, then glanced up at Gameknight999. There was so much anger and resentment in the boy's gaze, it nearly hurt to look back.

Kahn made a grumbling sound deep in his throat, causing rings of smoke to trickle out of his tiny nostrils. His clawed hands began to glow with a faint purple light as the magic around the creature grew in power; he was definitely getting ready to attack.

Gameknight looked down at Weaver and gave the boy a smile, then pulled Weaver behind him. The young NPC tried to complain, but Gameknight stilled his objections with a gentle hand on his shoulder.

"No one's gonna hurt you ever again, Weaver," Gameknight said. "I refuse to allow it!"

The User-that-is-not-a-user then grabbed Herder by the arm and did the same.

"These are all my friends, demon," the User-that-is-not-a-user snapped as he glared at Kahn. "Every creature out here is my friend and is under *my* protection. You'll have to go through me first before you can touch any of them."

"Sooo be it."

Balls of purple flame grew in the creature's hands. They became brighter and brighter as they grew in size.

Gameknight tensed. Dropping his iron sword, he pulled out the steeleaf shield Empech had made him. The remnants of the ice shards still protruded from the surface, their razor-sharp edges glinting in the sunlight.

Everything grew quiet. Gameknight heart pounded in his chest like a thundering funeral drum.

The demon drew his muscular arm back slowly, ready to launch the ball of magical flames at his target.

Beads of sweat trickled down Gameknight's face. Some of the salty drops tumbled into his eyes and stung a bit. He felt burning hot, and yet at the same time freezing cold. Waves of fear rippled through his body, making the User-that-is-not-a-user shake ever so slightly as he raised his shield. He braced himself for the blast of fire that would likely erase him from the face of Minecraft.

But then suddenly, a loud, piercing screech cut through the tense air.

"These are friends," Deimos said. The tiny fire-imp moved out from behind Digger. She shoved passed the terrified Mogs and Glugs, then stepped in front of Gameknight999.

"A fire-imp?!" the monster exclaimed in shock, confusion replacing the look of anger on its terrifying red face. "I sensed yourrr presence, but thought it waaas an echo of the immmps that once liiived in these laaaands."

"I am the last, and these people rescued me from the clutches of King Iago," Deimos growled. The little monster stepped forward and glared up at the gigantic demon. "They saved my life, and now all of these villagers and cave-dwellers are under *my* protection. If you will destroy anyone, you must start with me."

The tiny monster stared up at the huge demon, tendrils of smoke leaking from her nose and mouth. She took a step closer and glared up at the towering monster, Deimos' eyes glowing bright.

The red demon looked down at the little fire-imp, then glanced at Gameknight999 and his companions, then brought his terrifying gaze back down upon the fire-imp. Columns of smoke rose from the corners of his mouth, then slowly wrapped around his razor sharp tusks like ethereal wispy snakes.

Gameknight gripped his sword firmly, ready to leap in front of Deimos, but then relaxed as the purple flames in the monster's hands slowly shrunk down and were extinguished. With a nod, Kahn pulled in his wings and folded them against his back.

"If they arrre friends of yourrrs, little imp, thennn I will allow themmm to pass unharmed," the demon said slowly in his melodic voice.

"No, you will do even *more* than that," Deimos commanded, her voice edged with courage. "As the last fire-imp, I am now ruler of the imp-nation, and I order you to help us. You are a fire demon, just as I am. Granted, you have consumed a lot of magic and have grown big, but that does not release you from your obligation to our people. For flame and blood, you will help me right the wrongs perpetrated against our people. For flame and blood, you will obey my commands. For flame and blood, you will aid us in our cause."

The huge demon stepped forward, moving right up to Deimos. Gameknight tensed. Then the massive monster knelt before Deimos.

"For flammme annnd blood, this firrre demonnn will do as you commmmand," Kahn said, his deep voice making the very ground shake. "What issss it you commmmand?"

Deimos turned and glanced up at Gameknight999 expectantly.

"We need to get up into the trees," the User-that-is-not-a-user said. "Those nets must be brought down so we can get everyone up into the trees. We must bring this war to the sky. *You* are going to help us."

The monster stood and glanced at Gameknight999. Slowly, the User-that-is-not-a-user put away his weapons, then motioned for the others to do the same. Kahn then looked down at the fire-imp and nodded his terrifying head.

"I willl help youuu, little sisterrr," the demon said. "Kahn willll get youuu to the cloudssss."

"Good," Gameknight said. "We need to get up into those trees, fast, before Iago sends more reinforcements."

The tall demon scanned the collection of villagers. His eyes settled on Weaver, then on Herder. Weaver turned from the Kahn and glanced at Herder. He had an angry look on his square face, his eyes filled with jealousy and distrust. Kahn saw the look and shook his terrifying head.

"What mussst be donnne, mussst be donnne togeth-errr," Kahn growled. "Thesssse two willll not worrrk together. Kahn cannn see it innnn their eyessss." He turned and faced Gameknight999. "I cannot flyyy with annny other pair, annnd a single warrrrior will not beeee enough."

Weaver glanced at Herder, then looked up at Gameknight999. The User-that-is-not-a-user could see the emotional struggle within the boy. He wanted to reach out and comfort him, but before the User-that-is-not-a-user could move, Weaver began to speak.

"We can do this . . . me and Herder," the young boy said, the expression on his face changing from that of resentment to determination. "We'll lower the nets so all of you can get up into the treetops."

He glanced to Herder again, then turned and looked at Thea and Thorin, their muscular frames towering over the other NPCs. By now, more of the cave-dwellers were emerging from the tunnel to stand amongst the rest of the army. Gameknight watched as Weaver scanned all of the faces around him, then nodded almost imperceptibly. Standing tall, the blue-eyed boy moved to Herder's side. One of the wolves growled, uncertain about Weaver's intentions; the animals had always felt the tension between the two youths. But Herder held out a blocky hand to the animal, then reached up and placed a hand on Weaver's shoulder.

"There's no reason why we should be competitors," Herder said. "I'd prefer we were friends instead."

"Me too," Weaver agreed. "I'm sorry I've treated you so poorly. It's not your fault I'm mad at Smithy . . . I mean Gameknight999."

The User-that-is-not-a-user shifted uncomfortably from one foot to the other.

Weaver moved a step closer to the tall demon. "We're ready to do this. If you have a plan, me and Herder are ready."

Squawk! Tux added.

The alpha wolf barked in agreement.

Kahn glanced from Herder to Weaver, then smiled a wide, toothy smile that made everyone cringe involuntarily in fear, though it was probably meant to be friendly. The red demon laughed a loud, grumbly belly laugh that echoed through the forest.

"I knooow just whaaat to dooo," the monster said, then laughed again.

Gameknight glanced at the demon, then tilted his head back and stared up at the leafy canopy overhead.

This is gonna be dangerous, Gameknight thought. *I hope I'm not sending my two friends into something they can't handle.*

Have faith, child, an ancient, familiar voice said in his head.

The User-that-is-not-a-user turned and glanced about, looking for the Oracle, but of course she wasn't here. In fact, in this new timeline, the Oracle didn't seem to even exist at all.

Then how did I just hear her voice in my head? he thought.

No more words floated through his head other than his own.

"That was weird," the User-that-is-not-a-user muttered.

"What?" Hunter asked.

"Nothing, let's just get this done before it's too late."

"Excelllllent," Kahn said. "It's timmme to fly."

The demon reached out and wrapped an arm around each boy, then extended his wings. Gameknight and Deimos stepped back, as did the wolves. Kahn bent his knees, then cast the User-that-is-not-a-user another toothy smile and leapt into the air. In seconds, he was gone from sight.

CHAPTER 26

TO THE TREES

Suddenly, a streak of red flashed by just below the branches and leaves high overhead. Gameknight tried to follow Kahn's path, but the fire demon was just too fast. Up in the treetops, he could see feet moving, the troops preparing for something.

"Everyone, get ready," Gameknight said softly. "As soon as the nets come down, we must move fast."

The rest of the cave-dweller army was now emerging from the dark tunnel. There were hundreds of them, each holding a stone sword, some wielding axes and picks. They grumbled and growled excitedly.

Just then, Kahn streaked by again. He dove low, brushing the ground as he picked up speed, then shot straight up. With Herder and Weaver holding tight, he crashed through the foliage like a deadly red missile. Shouts of alarm floated down through the green canopy, followed by the clash of iron. The wolves paced back and forth, gazing upward and growling. Some of them began to howl; Gameknight wasn't sure if they were urging Herder on, or if they had sensed something terribly sad.

Just then, explosions rocked the treetops, causing leaves to flutter down to the ground like soft green rain.

Another blast shook the green canopy, causing more leaves to sprinkle to the ground, but this time, shouts of pain and fear punctuated the blast. More explosions, one after the other, shook the forest in rapid succession, the sounds nearly deafening.

And then, everything became eerily quiet.

Gameknight's entire body tensed, every nerve feeling electrified with fear. His heart pounded in his chest, beating faster and faster. Breaths of air rasped through his body in short gasps as terrible thoughts of *what if* filled his mind. The silence was deafening . . . and terrifying.

"Are they OK?" Stitcher said in a quiet, worried voice.

"I don't know," The User-that-is-not-a-user replied, his voice barely a whisper.

"What if they're . . . you know . . ." she asked, not wanting even to say it.

Gameknight couldn't respond. He couldn't even consider that option. If they were hurt, or worse, then he'd . . .

Suddenly, the cave-dwellers cheered. It was a deep, guttural roar that sounded more like a growl. The sound made Gameknight jump in fear, his nerves stretched to their limits.

"What is it?" Gameknight asked. "What is it?"

"Your two boys did it," Thorin grumbled. He pointed to one of the silvery webs slowly descending from the treetops. "The nets . . . they are being lowered."

Another net began to descend from the next tree, the filaments sparkling in the morning light.

Finally, Gameknight exhaled. He realized that he'd been holding his breath, and now he could breathe once again, the muscles in his arms and legs slowly releasing their clenched hold on his body.

A banging sound filled the air, someone hitting a sword or pickaxe against a chest plate. It was an alarm, perhaps a call for reinforcements. More explosions filled the air, father away. Gameknight could see the drizzle of leaves in the distance, the fluttering green rain marking the location of the blasts.

"Hurry everyone," the User-that-is-not-a-user said. "We need to get up there and help Weaver and Herder."

He took off running, a storm of Mogs and Glugs following behind. Jumping into the nearest net, Gameknight drew his diamond sword and held it close to his chest as the others crowded next to him. Crafter stood next to him, his eyes filled with trepidation.

"I'm sure they're okay," Gameknight said.

Crafter grunted, but neither of them were very certain.

Suddenly, the net shot up into the air. Gameknight held the gossamer strands tight as they ascended. Overhead, blocks of leaves were pulled aside as they neared the treetops, the opening filling with light. And then, in the blink of an eye, they were through the leafy barrier. The morning sun blasted down upon them, momentarily blinding all of the net-riders, especially the cave-dwellers. Gameknight shielded his eyes against the glare until his eyes adjusted. The net then dumped them to the ground on the sky island.

As he stood, the User-that-is-not-a-user glanced around, his sword held at the ready.

"About time you made it up here," Weaver said with a smile. "What took you so long?"

A howl cut through the air. Nearby, Herder was releasing a net filled with his wolves and a company of Mogs. He turned and waved, then lowered the net for another group of cave-dwellers. In the distance, the bright red form of Kahn was visible streaking across the treetops, purple balls of fire streaking down at the tree-dwellers who were foolish enough to stand their ground against the fire demon.

Off to the left, a stream of tree-dwellers shot into the air, their dirty and torn smocks looking all the more haggard as they landed on the sparkling sky island that hovered overhead. From across the treetops, they were fleeing, escaping into the sky from the army of cave-dwellers that was quickly spreading out across the green canopy.

In minutes, the treetops were completely occupied by the Mogs and Glugs, their green bodies blending in with the leaves, making them hard to spot in the distance. That was good; it would make their numbers hard to estimate.

"We need to hurry and get up there before Iago can prepare for us," Gameknight said, pointing to the sky island.

"How do we reach the floating lands overhead?" Thorin growled.

"There are blocks that will send us up in the air, but it only works one at a time."

Gameknight drew his swords and ran across the leaves until he found the green clay structure. Nearly all of the tree-dwellers were gone. The few that remained had either surrendered, or were just balls of XP littering the forest roof. The User-that-is-not-a-user explained how the catapult blocks worked, then had a group of Mogs pass the word to the other cave-dwellers.

"No doubt there will be warriors waiting for us," Gameknight said. "I think I should go first . . ."

But before the User-that-is-not-a-user could say another word, Thorin and Thea stepped up to the block.

"Come with me, wife," the big Mog growled.

With their arms around each other, they stepped onto the glowing block. Instantly, they were shot high into the air, landing gracefully on the sky island that floated overhead. The sounds of battle suddenly filling the air.

"Come on!" Gameknight shouted.

He stepped onto the block and streaked upward, likely into a fever-pitched battle against overwhelming numbers. But as he soared through the air, the User-that-is-not-a-user worried about his friends. He wasn't here to fight a war; he was here to catch Entity303. But deep down inside, Gameknight999 knew they had to do what's right, and that was to help the Mogs and Glugs.

As he rose, the User-that-is-not-a-user gripped his swords firmly and readied himself for battle.

CHAPTER 27

IAGO STRIKES BACK

"**W**hat do you mean, 'They're attacking'?!" King Iago screamed. "They're just a bunch of filthy cave-dwellers. I thought I told you to send the fallen-knights to destroy them."

The general took a step back. His mask was a pearly-white. Tiny rubies and emeralds embedded on the front and sides made it sparkle in the sunlight streaming through the windows, his long flowing green smock trimmed with colorful stitching.

"The fallen-knights were destroyed . . . sire."

"DESTROYED?!" Iago stood from his throne with fists clenched and glanced about the chamber, stunned. "How could they have defeated the fallen-knights? They're just cave-dwellers!"

"They were armed and organized, my liege," the general explained, taking another step back. "They all had stone swords, and their numbers were much bigger than we ever suspected. And . . ."

The general paused. He gave the door a wanting glance, then cast his gaze across the king's guards. The black-robed warriors stood absolutely motionless, as if they were statues. Their white masks were all directed at him, the dark eye holes in the masks looking threatening and dangerous.

"And . . . what?" the king demanded.

"Well, we had . . . uh . . . reports from the tree-dwellers, that . . . ah . . ."

"Just spit it out, you fool!"

"Well, they said a villager seemed to be leading them," the general finally explained.

"A villager?" Iago exclaimed. "How can that be? I exterminated all the villagers on the forest floor decades ago."

"They said the NPC was actually using two swords, sire," the general added.

"What?!" Iago glanced to Entity303, who was standing nearby.

"I told you not to underestimate Gameknight999," Entity303 murmured.

"Well, you need to do something about it," the ruler said, tiny beads of sweat leaking out from under his golden mask and staining the red collar that trimmed his purple smock.

"It appears you're sweating, Iago," the user said with a smile. "You'll need to change your clothing soon, before it becomes too soiled and dirty. After all, you know what happens to sky-dwellers who don't keep up their appearances." He laughed, then pointed out the window toward the trees below. "They become tree-dwellers."

Iago glared at the user, his eyes shining with anger.

"They must be stopped," the king bellowed. "The cave-dwellers cannot be allowed to rebel against my rule. Entity303, if you want your rocket complete, you must go down there and stop them."

"Don't be a fool, Iago," Entity303 replied.

The insult caused the dark-robed guards to shift their gaze from the general to Entity303, many of them reaching for their swords.

"Iago, tell your little pets to put away their swords before I punish a few of them."

The king waved the guards back, but many still kept their hands on their sword hilts.

"I will help you, not because I like you, but because I dislike Gameknight999," Entity303 said.

"What will you do?" Iago asked. "Will you lead a company of my soldiers down to the forest floor and defeat them?"

"Of course not," the user replied. "You need not go down to them. They will come up here. All you need do is destroy Gameknight999 and the rabble will be leaderless and crumble. We will set a trap that not even the great User-that-is-not-a-user can escape. Then, that pesky meddler will be exterminated, and you can get back to destroying the cave-dwellers, and I can get back to my rocket."

Suddenly, a masked citizen threw open the doors and bolted into the room. He was shabbily dressed, with an orange mask that was scratched and stained, and a blue cloak that was dirty and tattered. He panted as if he'd just sprinted to get to the king. Clearly, it was a tree-dweller.

"They're on the treetops," he said. "The cave-dwellers are on the treetops!"

"This is all impossible," Iago growled, shocked and angry.

"I told you, Gameknight999 will come to you," Entity303 said. "And once he is destroyed, it'll be easy enough to destroy the rest. I'll take care of everything, but . . ."

"But what?" Iago asked.

"But I don't see anyone running out to work on my rocket." Entity303 moved to a window and peeked out at the distant building. "I should see the nose cone sticking up out of the roof, and yet there's nothing. Maybe I should go work on the rocket myself instead of setting the trap for the villagers?"

"No, no, it will be taken care of," Iago said. "Othello, where are you?"

"Here, sire," the assistant replied, stepping out of the shadows.

"Have the engineers finish the rocket and see that it is fueled and fully provisioned."

"Yes, sire," Othello replied.

The assistant ran off, pushing his way through the tall, white-masked guards.

Entity303 smiled.

"Excellent," the user said. "Now, this is what we're going to do . . ."

And as Entity303 explained his trap, king Iago stopped pacing back and forth and began chuckling an evil, maniacal laugh, his eyes shining with hatred for his attackers.

CHAPTER 28

REVOLUTION

Gameknight pushed the masked warriors back, jabbing at them with his iron sword, then swung his diamond blade with all his strength. It hit one enemy in front of him on the shoulder, causing his ornately decorated smock to tear, revealing chainmail underneath. The warrior hissed, his eyes turning momentarily bright silver through the eye holes of his dark brown mask, then he lunged. Stepping aside, Gameknight let the soldier fall clumsily to the ground as he overextended his reach, letting those behind him finish the enemy off.

"Everyone push forward!" the User-that-is-not-a-user shouted.

The Mogs and Glugs growled in agreement and shoved the sky-dwellers back, their razor-sharp claws slicing through smocks only to reveal more chainmail. Shouts of pain came from the masked soldiers, but also from the cave-dwellers as casualties were taken on both sides of the battle line.

They were fighting across a grassy courtyard, the grass a bright red. A few trees dotted the landscape, their dark trunks standing out against the shining silver leaves. A low cobblestone wall ringed the edge of the island, with torches spaced along the stone barrier to provide light in the evening. On the other side of the courtyard stood a lavish home, multiple stories high. Colored glass adorned the windows that covered the stone- and emerald-lined walls, with quartz-block balconies jutting out of the walls like bony protrusions.

The User-that-is-not-a-user marveled at the construction, but sensed the wastefulness in it. Slaves had likely been used to build this thing, and then been cast aside when it was completed and the manpower was no longer needed. The wastefulness of all this wealth when people lived in poverty below made his blood boil.

Glancing over his shoulder, Gameknight saw his friends were now on the sky island. Herder's wolves were spreading out like a furry white flood, snapping at arms and legs with their powerful jaws. Hunter and Stitcher stood atop a wall and fired down at the masked opponents, the *Flame* enchantment on their bows instantly lighting their arrows ablaze. Crafter and Weaver moved to Gameknight's side, their swords flashing through the air like iron lightning, while Digger stayed back to protect the pechs and Tux.

A continual flow of Mogs and Glugs were now coming up through the hole, riding the burst of speed delivered by the catapult block on the treetops below. Like a flowing green wave, they crashed down upon the defenders, their eyes glowing bright red with anger at their oppressors.

Suddenly, one of the wolves howled in pain as a pair of arrows struck the creature. The wolf yelped as it struggled to stand, then a third arrow took the last of its HP. The wolf disappeared with a sad, lonely howl. Herder stared up at the balcony that ringed the building they were approaching. Archers were slowly filling the space, their sharp-pointed shafts raining down upon the cave-dwellers. The lanky boy growled as he stared up at the archers, then used his sword to bat an arrow out of the sky that was heading toward him.

"Wolves, hunt the archers!" Herder yelled. "Let none survive!"

"Herder, don't you think that's a bit extreme?" Gameknight asked.

The young boy glared at his friend, his eyes filled with rage; he was lost to the fever of battle. Weaving between combatants, he ran off to follow the wolves. Crafter moved forward and took the boy's place, his sword driving back the other masked swordsmen.

Just then, Thorin and Thea both let out a deep, guttural growl and charged forward. The massive creatures crashed into the enemy line, knocking their adversaries aside as if they were bowling pins, the pair of monsters like green fanged-and-clawed bowling balls. The soldiers tried to get back into formation, but more of the cave-dwellers were arriving every minute. Across the sky, Gameknight could see the creatures streaking up into the air and landing on distant sky islands; the revolution was spreading.

The soldiers charged forward, hoping to push them back and seal off the sky island. Suddenly, more archers appeared on a large balcony, a mossy cobblestone wall ringing the edge of the structure.

"Hunter, Stitcher . . . the balcony," Gameknight said, pointing with this diamond sword.

Flaming arrows streaked through the air and hit the masked soldiers, but the return fire was far more than the two sisters could handle. They ducked for cover as lethal projectiles rained down from above. A flaming ball of purple fire flashed through the air and struck the balcony. It exploded, tearing a massive hole in the floor, dumping the warriors to the ground. Another ball of fire struck the survivors, then exploded, ripping away the last of their HP.

A loud thud sounded from behind Gameknight999. He turned and found Kahn standing behind him, a strangely satisfied look on his terrifyingly demonic face.

"That's howww you take carrre of pests," he growled.

Before the User-that-is-not-a-user could reply, Kahn leapt up into the sky, looking for more targets of opportunity. Explosive balls of fire hammered away at the defenders, forcing them to duck for cover, letting the cave-dwellers close the distance and fall upon the soldiers.

They ran to the massive building, archers firing down at them from higher floors. Herder's wolves darted about, snapping at anything they could reach while dodging arrows. The Mogs and Glugs were less careful. They just barreled toward any enemy they spotted, their stone swords held proudly in the air.

Gameknight carefully opened the doors to the structure and peeked in. An arrow zipped past his head, barely missing him. He ducked back and started formulating a new plan when a group of Glugs charged into the building. They smashed through the doors, heedless of the arrows that fell down upon them from the defenders. Gameknight and Herder slipped in behind them, three of his wolves at the lanky boy's side. Atop the curving staircase, a group of archers fired down at them. The warriors ducked into doorways when Gameknight fired back.

A squad of Mogs now entered the room and charged up the stairs. Instantly, the archers turned and fled through the many passages that extended throughout the building, the corridors like elaborately decorated arteries. Gameknight and Herder ran up the steps and sprinted down the nearest passage. It led into a gigantic bedroom, replete with a chandelier and many stained-glass windows. One wall was covered with wooden chests, enough to hold items for an entire village . . . or army. At the far side stood a large group of archers, arrows notched and pointing at the doorway.

The enemy archers used furniture in the bedroom as a barricade, hiding behind beds and tables to fire at the entrance. Just when Gameknight was about to charge into the room and face a hail of arrows, Kahn smashed through the back of the house. He was a bright red battering ram, shredding the wall with ease. The soldiers, caught by surprise, just stood there in shock, gazing at the massive demon. But then one of them fired an arrow at Kahn; that was a mistake. With a flick of his wing, he knocked the arrow out of the air, then sent a barrage of purple fireballs down upon the defenders. The balls of flame crashed into the warriors, smashing walls and floors, dumping them to the ground. When the soldiers tried to stand, they found themselves completely surrounded by cave-dwellers. Those who wanted to live surrendered quickly, while those who held to their racist beliefs that cave-dwellers were beneath them and refused to give up were quickly destroyed.

Gameknight stepped to the open wall and looked out across the sky island. Green bodies were visible everywhere as the cave-dwellers surged across the land. Many sky-dwellers threw their weapons to the ground and begged for mercy; these were taken prisoner and put in a holding pen that Digger was still carving into the ground. Some of the warriors refused to surrender, and fled the island using their Elytra wings. Others found the catapult block on the far end and shot up into the air, gliding to the massive island nearby that held Iago's glittering castle.

"That's where we're going next," Gameknight said to Herder, pointing toward the castle.

One of the wolves next to him howled, causing the rest of the animals to join in, adding their majestic voices to the song. Some of the Mogs and Glugs below heard the echoing call and joined in, the sound from the island growing louder and louder until it was like a klaxon, blaring their melody of freedom across the landscape.

"Well, look what we have here," a voice said behind them.

Gameknight turned and found Hunter searching some of the chests lined up against the wall. She reached in and pulled out countless Elytra wings. Moving to the next chest, she opened it and lifted more of the delicate wings from the wooden box.

"These are all full of Elytra," the redhead said.

"Good. Gather them all; we'll need them," Gameknight said.

He moved to an undamaged window and peered out across the world. Sky-dwellers were fighting on every island, the flood of green Mogs and Glugs flowing relentlessly across each. Many of the masked citizens were taking to the air, flying away from their doomed little kingdoms, seeking refuge on other islands or gliding down to the trees below.

But then Gameknight noticed something in the distance. It was a metallic thing reflecting the bright sunlight, sticking up through the roof of a large, cobblestone structure. He instantly recognized it: it was the nose cone of a rocket. Just beyond, he could see sky islands with geysers of oil shooting up into the air. One had a complicated-looking thing built next to the oil well. After following the series of pipes and containers, Gameknight realized what it was . . . a refinery.

"So that's what you're up to, Entity303," Gameknight said, nodding in understanding.

"What?" Hunter asked, following his gaze.

"You see that island with all the pipes and tubes built around the oil well?" Gameknight asked, pointing off into the distance. "That's a refinery. Entity303 is building a rocket, and he's using Iago's workers to fuel it with that oil."

"A rocket?" Herder asked, moving to his side. "What do you mean?"

"That thin metallic spire sticking up through the roof of that cobblestone building, that's the nose cone of a rocket," the User-that-is-not-a-user explained. "Entity303 must be trying to go to space, for some reason, and he's convinced King Iago to help him."

"Remember the rocket motors?" Hunter said. "Iago was adding rocket engines to all the sky islands to keep them in the air. That's probably what he's getting from Entity303."

Gameknight grunted, lost in thought for a moment. "We need to get to that rocket as quickly as possible."

"To do that, we'll need to go through Iago's personal island," Hunter said.

"You can be sure there will be more soldiers there . . . and more fighting," Stitcher said. The girl had entered the room quietly and was now standing at her sister's side.

"Good," Hunter added.

"Bring all those Elytra wings," Gameknight said. "We need to move, fast."

"Alright!" the redheads exclaimed.

I just hope Entity303 doesn't have any surprises waiting for us, Gameknight thought.

He grabbed an armful of Elytra and ran down the stairs, heading for the far end of the island and his enemy, Entity303.

CHAPTER 29

AERIAL COMBAT

Gameknight distributed the Elytra wings to everyone and showed the cave-dwellers how to use them. They barely fit onto their huge bodies, but, once adjusted, seemed to become part of them.

"I wish we had more time to show your people how to use these," Gameknight said to Thorin.

"We are Mogs and Glugs," the green cave-dweller replied in a deep, rumbling voice. "We will adapt, or we will die. Either choice is better than slavery."

"Well, that's cheery," Hunter replied with a sarcastic smile, slapping the big Mog on the shoulder.

He gave her a toothy grin that was part humorous and part terrifying, then he patted her on the shoulder, accidently knocking her to the ground. The cave-dwellers laughed their guttural laugh as Thorin reached down and helped Hunter to her feet.

"Be careful, husband," Thea chided.

Thorin just shrugged.

"Just remember everyone: When you get to the highest point, lean forward and the wings will open," Gameknight said for the third time. "Now watch me and I'll show you . . ."

Thorin pushed past the User-that-is-not-a-user and stepped on the glowing catapult block. He was instantly fired into the air. He passed through a cloud and was then gone from sight.

"Does anyone see him?" Digger said. "Where did he go?"

Just then, a low, growling sound percolated out of the cloud. At first, Gameknight thought the cave-dweller was screaming in terror; it was difficult to tell with the Mogs and Glugs. But then Thorin shot out of the cloud with the gray wings extended, a gigantic smile on his green face. He wasn't screaming; he was laughing with joy.

The other cave-dwellers saw the look on Thorin's face and all pushed toward the edge of the sky-island, shooting up into the air, looks of childlike wonder on their faces.

"EVERYONE, FOLLOW ME!" Gameknight shouted as he shot up into the air.

The wind rushed past him as he soared higher and higher, thrown into the air by the orange-glowing catapult block, his friends following close behind. Instantly, Kahn was at the User-that-is-not-a-user's side, his dark wings riding delicately on the air currents. Gameknight banked and headed for Iago's distant island as a group of sky-dwellers emerged from a cloud. They were formed in a tight "V" formation, bows in their hands and arrows notched. At the head of the enemy formation was a soldier wearing a bright red smock with jagged white lines adorning the sides.

"Enemies coming in," Hunter warned, pointing to their opponents.

"Hunter, Stitcher, aim for their leader," Gameknight shouted over the rush of the wind.

Flaming arrows streaked across the sky, seeking the warrior in bright red. His face was a dark red mask, like the color of dried blood. It made Gameknight shudder for a moment, but he shrugged aside the fear and concentrated on the task at hand.

Arrows streaked back and forth, but with the blast of the wind and their speeds, it was difficult to hit anything. Gameknight knew he could not match the skill of the sisters anyway, and his arrows would just be wasted. Instead, he put away his bow and drew his two swords. Leaning forward, he accelerated toward the red menace, a pair of Mogs forming up on either side.

"Stay with the group!" Crafter shouted, but Gameknight ignored him.

He could tell the red warrior was the leader of the aerial forces by the way he flew. If he could take him out, then the rest of the flyers would be leaderless and would likely scatter.

Picking up speed, the User-that-is-not-a-user glanced at the green monsters on either side. They took to flying incredibly quickly and were now in a tight V-formation, with Gameknight at the tip.

The red warrior saw them coming and fired an arrow at him. Gameknight swatted it away with his diamond blade. Another arrow came streaking toward them, zipping through the center of their formation, but this one hit one of the green creatures to his left. The creature growled in pain and dropped his stone sword, but did not waver a bit from the formation. Long black claws extended from the creature's fingertips. They sparkled in the light of the sun, making them appear even sharper and more lethal.

Suddenly, another wing of masked warriors were above them, materializing from out of a thick, white cloud while a third group appeared off to their right. They all drew swords and dove toward Gameknight and his four Mog companions.

"Faster!" Gameknight shouted.

They leaned into the dive, hoping to reach the red-masked leader before the other two groups descended upon them. The distance closed between Gameknight and his adversary as the wind screamed in his ears. He could now see the red warrior's eyes shining like silvery coins through the eye slots. *Strange how they seem so familiar,* he thought.

Gameknight and his green companions went faster, the fabric of their Elytra wings straining to stay in one piece. Another group of soldiers banked toward them, their smocks fluttering in with the wind. Concerned expressions began to cover the square faces of the Mogs, their red eyes darting from one group of enemies to the next. The anger at their oppressors was slowly being replaced by an all-too-familiar emotion . . . fear.

They were now surrounded and heading straight toward the crimson flyer and his warriors. Gameknight thought about World War I and all the pilots who had gone after the Red Baron. He hoped he would fare better.

As they closed, the masked soldiers put away their bows and drew swords; so the battle was to be hand-to-hand combat. Gameknight smiled, then gripped the handle of his blades firmly.

"Mogs, go attack that group of warriors," Gameknight said, pointing to the closest group of fighters to the right. "I'll take care of the group in front of me."

"But we are outnumbered," one of the Mogs cried out in concern. "We should not split up. This battle seems impossible. We should head for the trees."

"If we quit, we guarantee the outcome," the User-that-is-not-a-user said in a loud, clear voice. "This is a battle for the freedom of the cave-dwellers and the safety of Minecraft. We can do this, as long as we work together. Help will arrive; now break off and attack!"

The Mogs growled in agreement, then banked away and headed toward the other wing of soldiers.

Gameknight leaned forward and sped up. His target's eyes now glowed with a silvery luster. The red flyer was getting closer and closer. They were heading directly at each other. In seconds, they would crash.

Just before impact, Gameknight dove slightly, then rolled over onto his back and protected his wings.

Reaching up with his swords, he slashed at the red warrior's Elytra as they passed within a hair's breadth of each other. The warrior's sword dug into Gameknight's shoulder, but he ignored the pain. Instead, he smiled as he felt his blades slice through the warrior's wings.

The red soldier's eyes turned from anger to terror as the wings folded up, then splintered apart. With a loud, terrified scream, the warrior plummeted to the ground, his silver eyes staring back at Gameknight in sudden panic and fear.

A sword clanked against his diamond boot, pulling his awareness from the doomed flying and back to those pursuing him. Gameknight banked hard to the right, trying to escape those still following him, but they were right on his tail. Leaning forward, he traded altitude for speed as he streaked for a cloud. Suddenly, the air was alive with arrows, some of the shafts aflame. The projectiles hit the warriors following on his heels, shredding their wings and sticking into their backs like porcupine quills. They fell from the sky as if swatted by some kind of giant flyswatter. The warriors' screams pierced the air as they tumbled downward.

Crafter emerged from the glare of the sun, leading a group of Glug flyers to Gameknight's side, then fell into formation around him.

"You having fun out here?" Hunter shouted, her voice just barely audible over the wind.

"Well, I was . . ." Gameknight began.

"Here come some more!" Crafter yelled.

Off to the left, a large group of Iago's warriors dove right at them. There were at least thirty in the squadron, if not more. But then a collection of Mogs appeared out of a boxy cloud. They were in no formation to speak of, just a large collection of green bodies, the gray wings on their backs straining with their weight. The cave-dwellers didn't even draw their swords. Instead, the green creatures extended dark, razor-sharp claws and growled. They smashed into the soldiers, slashing at wings and crashing into enemy bodies. Many on both sides fell, but the masked warriors, unaccustomed to creatures that would fight back, were not prepared for the cave-dwellers' ferocity. They were quickly wiped from the sky.

"Come on, everyone form up tight on me," Gameknight yelled. He slowed to allow the others to catch up. "We're going to Iago's palace. You can be sure he'll have archers there waiting for us, so we're going in fast. Don't slow until the last instant. When you hit the ground, move . . . don't stand still. Does everyone understand?"

The Mogs and Glugs all made low, guttural growls that made the sky sound as if it were filled with thunder.

"OK, LET'S FLY!"

Gameknight leaned forward and sped up. Suddenly, a howl filled the air off to the right. Glancing toward the sound, the User-that-is-not-a-user saw a group of Mogs holding Herder's wolves. The animals could sense the impending battle and were howling their battle cry. Weaver joined the concert and howled, followed by Herder and Hunter. And then suddenly all of them were howling with the wolves. They were one army, streaking toward unknown forces, howling the pride in their cause and in their might.

"HERE WE COME, ENTITY303!" Gameknight shouted. "A-OOOOOO!"

CHAPTER 30

TRAPPED

He reached the red grass of Iago's massive floating island flying at full speed. Gameknight pulled back at just the last instant, reducing his speed so that he wouldn't crash. When his feet touched the crimson grass, he rolled across the ground, shedding his wings and donning his diamond chest plate, then drew his enchanted sword and steeleaf shield. Charging straight toward a group of archers, the User-that-is-not-a-user yelled at the top of his lungs as he kept the shield over his head. Arrows thudded against the shield like machine gun fire, some of the pointed shafts going all the way through and sticking through the back, stopping just inches from his face.

With the archers focusing on him, the rest of the army was able to land with fewer enemies firing at them. The cave-dwellers landed with *thud*s, many of them falling over and taking damage from landing too fast, but they just leapt right back to their feet and charged at their oppressors.

Instantly, Hunter and Stitcher placed blocks on the ground and fired from behind the stones, picking off snipers that hid in the silvery trees. Crafter drew his bow and added his own arrows to the assault, trying to get as many of the enemy archers as possible.

Herder's wolves were dropped to the ground by the cave-dwellers as they landed. The animals took off running, their howls adding to the cacophony of battle as they shot through the chaos like furry white missiles in search of masked targets.

With the Mogs and Glugs now on the ground, they all charged at the masked defenders. Their anger at their enemy was so great, they ignored the hail of arrows descending on them, and focused on destroying their persecutors. Many of the green giants disappeared during the assault, but it did not deter them; they knew this battle was being fought for their children, and nothing was going to stop them.

Soon, the landing field, which looked like a large park, complete with benches under silver trees and a trickling fountain in the middle, was clear of defenders. Colorful balls of XP littered the ground, each glowing a different color. Most were from the sky-dwellers that had been ordered to hold this land, but many piles of tiny, glowing spheres also had stone swords lying nearby. The butcher's bill had been steep; many had paid dearly on both sides of the battle.

Before Gameknight now stood the palace of King Iago. It was a massive construction, built from quartz and gold, with towers stretching up to the sky, turrets mounted atop an elaborately decorated wall, with great sweeping archways over dark passages. Stained glass windows dotted the upper floors, the light from within making them appear to glow. Looming high above everything was the palace's main structure. It was a gigantic cylinder made gold and quartz, with decorative designs of lapis and emerald spiraling up the sides. At the top of the tower was Iago's throne; that was where they'd likely find the king.

Gameknight gathered everyone together, then assigned where they would go. He had the Mogs enter the palace from the right-most archway, the Glugs using the left, while he and his friends would advance through the center.

"Everyone, GO!" the user-that-is-not-a-user shouted.

Hundreds of pairs of feet pounded across the floating island as they charged into Iago's castle. The central passage was dark, the torches likely extinguished by the retreating army. Crafter placed torches on the walls as they ran, lighting the way for any of the cave-dwellers still landing on the island.

Squawk! Tux said in a low, screechy voice, still held by Digger.

"Yeah, I'm scared too," Gameknight said. He reached out and patted the animal on the head. "This will all be over soon."

"I'm not sure I like the sound of that," Digger said, his voice wavering with fear.

"You know what I mean," the User-that-is-not-a-user said as he ran. "With the army of Mogs and Glugs, I don't think Iago has a chance. He must know that by now, and is figuring out a way to negotiate for peace. This will be a different world tomorrow."

Suddenly, the passage turned and opened to a gigantic courtyard. It was massive, spanning nearly the entire width of the sky island. A wall of gold at least twenty blocks high ringed the area, with a balcony of cobblestone running along the perimeter. A roof of quartz extended over the terrace, shielding it from rain and the bright rays of the sun. Without any torches, the balcony was cloaked in shadows.

As Gameknight and his friends emerged from their tunnel, he cast an uneasy gaze up at the walkway overhead. Something about it didn't seem right. The Mogs and Glugs stepped out of their passages and looked about, expecting enemies; but all they saw was an empty courtyard filled with friends.

"Maybe they all ran away?" Hunter said, jokingly, though her face did not show any humor.

Her eyes darted about, looking for threats, her enchanted bow held at the ready. Cautiously, they all moved into the center of the square, looking for an exit.

At the far end of the courtyard was a quartz-lined passage, glowstone blocks embedded in the walls casting a warm yellow light on the interior.

"Over there," Digger said. "A passage."

"Right," Gameknight replied. "Come on everyone, we need to catch Iago and Entity303."

They ran toward the opening, but as soon as the entire army was within the massive courtyard, the ground began to shake. Blocks of sand fell across the opening to the passage, blocking their exit. Quickly, Gameknight turned around, checking the other tunnels. They too were now blocked by piles of sand . . . they were all trapped!

"What do we do?" Digger asked, panic in his voice.

Squawk! Tux added.

"Yes, what *do* you do?" an evil-sounding voice said from the balcony.

A torch flared into life, showing both King Iago and Entity303 staring down at them.

"You were correct, Entity303, the fools were certainly predictable. We led them right into this trap," Iago said.

"Yeah, Gameknight999 can't help himself," Entity303 said, smiling maliciously. "When he thinks he's doing a good deed, he'll chase just about anything."

"Bows!" Gameknight shouted.

The NPCs pulled out their bows and aimed at the king and user on the balcony.

"I'd be careful with those if I were you," Iago said. "ARCHERS!"

Suddenly, a string of torches flared into life all along the balcony that ringed the courtyard. The flickering light showed countless archers, each with bows in their hands, pointing down at Gameknight and his friends. Their multi-colored masks and ornately decorated smocks looked ominous in the torchlight as they glared down at the trapped intruders.

"I'd lower your weapons if I were you," Entity303 said with a mocking grin.

Gameknight lowered his bow and glared up at the user.

"It has been fun watching you chase me around, but I think it's time for me to leave you to your well-deserved fate," Entity303 turned to face Weaver. "You can still come with me, villager. I offer to spare your life, even if it is just to cause your friends pain."

"Never! I won't go anywhere with you ever again," Weaver snapped.

"Too bad, I was hoping you'd betray your friend, Smithy of the Two-Swords . . . or have you finally figured out he's really Gameknight999? . . . I know you aren't very bright. That user next to you probably won the Great Zombie Invasion because he took on the guise of Smithy. But I did enjoy watching your anger grow toward him because of his deceit. He probably hasn't told you that you were the key to letting me put all these mods into Minecraft, has he? Without you in the past, everything evolved along a different path. It doesn't really matter now. I doubt you'll be leaving this palace alive, so what you know about the future is insignificant. But, please, go on being mad at Gameknight999; I love watching the sadness on his square face."

Weaver glanced at Gameknight999, an expression of sudden regret and guilt in his bright, blue eyes.

"This isn't over, Entity303," Gameknight growled at the evil user.

He took a step forward. All of the archers above turned their bows toward him.

"You still think you have a chance?" the vile user asked. "Ha . . . what a laugh. You truly are a fool. Goodbye, Gameknight999. I have a flight to catch."

Entity303 moved off the balcony and into a dark passage behind him.

"It is time for this foolishness to end," King Iago said, his eyes now glowing with a silvery light. "The extinction of the cave-dwellers is about to begin."

He turned to face his warriors.

"Archers . . . ready."

Gameknight could hear a hundred bows creaking with strain as bowstrings were pulled taut. Panic and fear ruled his mind as beads of terrified sweat trickled down the back of his neck

"Aim . . ."

Some of them turned from Gameknight999 and chose another target, many of them aiming at the other NPCs. The User-that-is-not-a-user felt as if his nerves were all aflame, his heart pounding in his chest like a funeral drum.

Funny how everything feels so real and alive just before your own death, Gameknight thought.

"FIRE!"

CHAPTER 31

RED LIGHTNING

Just as the archers were about to release their arrows, a great roar boomed through the air. The walls of the palace shook and panes of stained glass cracked under the strain. It felt as if the entire world were falling apart. The soldiers held their shot as they looked around nervously, searching for the source of the thunderous sound.

A flash of red appeared at the top of the quartz roof that extended over the balcony. Suddenly, Deimos stepped to the edge of the overhang, screaming at the top of her voice.

"KING IAGO!"

The small fire-imp held out a hand and waited as a tiny ball of fire formed. She threw it at the king, the minute sphere of flame streaking through the air, only to fizzle out before it ever reached its target. All of the archers, instead of firing, laughed aloud, their chuckles muffled as they floated out from behind their colorful masks.

"You are guilty of destroying the fire-imp people," Deimos pronounced. "You purposely destroyed the red grass on which we fed, which destroyed the ecosystem of the forest floor. For these crimes, you have been found guilty and will now be punished."

The colorful ruler stopped laughing and glared at the tiny red creature.

"You dare interrupt these proceedings?" Iago said, his eyes glowing silvery bright with rage. "Archers, destroy the last fire-imp first, then fire at will at those in the courtyard. Leave none alive!"

The warriors turned their arrows toward Deimos, but the tiny fire-imp did not move. In fact, she stood a little taller, unafraid of the wave of pointed shafts about to descend upon her.

Suddenly, what appeared to be a flash of red lightning zipped through the air. Dark wings extended from the edges of the crimson streak, smashing into soldiers, and knocking many of them to the ground. Turning in a tight arc that seemed impossible at those speeds, Kahn suddenly stopped midair, hovering at the center of the courtyard. Before any of the soldiers could move, he launched balls of purple flame at the balconies, smashing the stone walkway and sending many of the soldiers tumbling to the ground below. Those who had not been knocked from the balcony turned their bows toward the red demon. They fired their pointed shafts at the monster, but Kahn was too fast. He beat his wings and flew high into the sky, then arced down again, smashing into the archers.

The NPCs on the ground scattered, firing up at Iago's remaining archers as the Mogs and Glugs attacked the soldiers who fell from the balconies. Many of the cave-dwellers dug their claws into the walls and began to climb, even under the hail of arrows. They easily reached the balcony, then threw themselves at the defenders.

A section of the wall near the back of the courtyard slowly slid open, revealing a hidden passage, out of which poured more foot soldiers, but they still stood no chance against the pent-up anger of the cave-dwellers. The green monsters crashed into the newcomers, all of them howling in terrible rage.

"Kahn, blast the sand that's blocking the exits," Gameknight shouted.

The red demon nodded his head, then flapped his wings and shot high into the air. With flicks of his wrist, he sent balls of magical fire at the piles of sand. The burning spheres exploded when they hit the pale obstacles, blasting apart the piles and tearing a huge hole in the palace wall.

"Come on, we must catch Entity303!" Gameknight shouted to his friends.

They ran for the exit, slashing at targets of opportunity as they zigzagged across the courtyard. When Gameknight reached the palace exit, he saw Iago sprinting across a narrow wooden bridge, heading to a small floating structure that hovered near his massive sky island. On the smaller island was the cobblestone building Gameknight had seen, the nose cone of the rocket sticking up through the roof. Nearby, a small island with a geyser of oil spouted up in the air. A series of pipes and mechanisms had been built around the oil, bringing the dark liquid into the building.

Iago sprinted across the wooden bridge, glancing back at his pursuers as he ran. The shining light in his eyes had faded, changing from an expression of rage to one of fear. Stopping in the middle of the bridge, he pulled out an axe and began to chop. The ruler broke block after block until he'd created a wide gap in the structure, too wide to jump across. Satisfied he was safe, the king waved at his pursuers, then dumped the blocks of wood into a nearby chest and ran into the building, where his black-clad guards were waiting for him.

Gameknight and the others sprinted to the bridge, but were stopped by the gap.

"We must get to that island," Crafter said. "Entity303 is probably over there."

"Don't you think I know that?" Gameknight snapped, then felt bad about his abrupt answer. "I'm sorry."

"It's OK, we're all under stress," Crafter said.

"Does anyone have anything to build with?" Digger asked.

They all shook their heads.

"I saw Iago put the wood from his demolition of the bridge in that chest over there," Stitcher said, pointing to the wooden box on the ground at the far end of the bridge. "If we can make it to that chest, then we'll be able to . . ."

"I can make the jump," Gameknight said. "Everyone back up."

"You can't make that jump, it's at least five blocks . . . " Hunter said. "A three block jump is hard enough, but five?"

There was an expression of fear on her face, as if she already knew that Gameknight was going to try anyway.

"I have one block, maybe it can help," Gameknight said.

"So what?" Hunter exclaimed in disbelief. "You just made it a four block jump . . . it's still impossible."

"I have to try."

Gameknight moved to the edge of the bridge. Directly below was darkness as the sun began to set behind the horizon to the west. Rays of crimson and orange bathed the landscape as the sun went further behind the horizon, the putrid green sky overhead fading to black.

And then he saw some of the Mogs flying toward the palace from the neighboring islands and had an idea. Instead of placing the block of dirt on the edge of the opening, reducing the gap from five to four, he placed it on the bridge, raising his height by one. He stood on the raised block, then removed his chest plate and put on his Elytra wings.

"That's not gonna work!" Hunter yelled, but Gameknight wasn't listening. "You won't have enough speed for the Elytra to hold you up." She took a step closer, fear etched on her face. "If you try to jump the gap, you'll fall through the hole and . . ." She couldn't finish the statement.

"I have to try," Gameknight replied.

The User-that-is-not-a-user stared at the tall metallic spire sticking out from the roof of the huge stone building, just a few blocks away. He had to get there, fast. Moving back to the edge of the dirt, he sprinted forward, taking one step, then another onto the raised block, and then jumped out into the open air.

Gravity would now determine his fate.

CHAPTER 32

LAUNCH PAD

I t felt like he was moving in slow motion. Gameknight jumped as high and as fast as he could. When he reached the apex of his leap, he leaned forward and opened his Elytra wings.

As first they fluttered and threatened to fold back up. Icicles of fear stabbed at his every nerve. *Am I gonna fall?* But then they stuck out straight and caught the wind. The wings held him aloft just long enough to allow him to float across the gap, just barely getting one foot on the opposite side. With a stumbling, clumsy landing, Gameknight crashed to the solid wooden bridge, breaking one of his wings on impact. It didn't matter. All that was important was catching Entity303 . . . wings could always be repaired later.

Throwing the Elytra aside, Gameknight quickly put on his armor and moved to the chest. Pulling out a stack of wood, he moved to the bridge and filled in the gap. As soon as the opening was partially repaired, the Mogs and Glugs began pouring across the bridge, everyone running toward the large stone building and metallic nose cone looming high in the air.

Gameknight handed the rest of the blocks to one of the Glugs, then turned and sprinted for the building.

As he ran, a loud hissing noise followed by the grinding of something metallic, maybe gears, filled the air. It was the sort of clatter one would expect from some kind of machine or a damaged carnival ride. More clanking and grinding could be heard behind the walls, followed by a scraping sound, as if something were being dragged across the ground.

The building before them was made of cobblestone that stretched maybe twenty blocks into the air. The wall was featureless, with no windows or openings, save for a set of iron doors set in the side of the structure, blocking their entrance. No lever or button was obviously visible.

"How are we gonna get in?" Weaver asked.

Before anyone could speak, a ball of purple flame from Kahn, somewhere behind them, streaked over their heads and struck the doors. Instantly, the sphere exploded, tearing the doors off their hinges and leaving behind a gaping hole in the wall.

Gameknight bolted through, his friends and army of cave-dwellers on his heels. The passage was dark, with no torches or glowstones to drive away the shadows. Someone stuck a torch on the wall behind him, casting a circle of flickering light, but as the User-that-is-not-a-user sprinted forward, he quickly outpaced the illumination and was in darkness again. The enchantments of his sword cast only the smallest amount of light around him, making the next step before him visible, but little else.

When he reached the end of the corridor, Gameknight moved into a large, well-lit atrium. Against one wall stood Iago's personal guards. The black-clad soldiers, with their ornately decorated white masks, stared menacingly at Gameknight999, their shining swords held at the ready.

The User-that-is-not-a-user skidded to a stop. A huge rocket ship sat on a launch pad, Entity303 at the door, about to step inside. King Iago was running toward him, yelling at the top of his lungs.

"You must take me with you," the masked ruler cried out desperately to Entity303. "The filthy cave-dwellers are destroying everything!"

Just then, a nearby sky-island moaned as cracks formed across its surface. Pieces of a large brick house crumbled as the fissure snaked across the structure, cutting it in two. The land then did the unthinkable; it began to sink downward. Beneath the floating land, Mogs and Glugs could be seen crawling along the underside, tearing at the levitation blocks with their sharp claws, leaping off the doomed island and floating to the ground on Elytra wings. Masked sky-dwellers screamed out in horror as they rode their doomed island to the forest below.

Across the darkening sky, more of the islands began to sink as the Mogs and Glugs destroyed the glowing blocks under the land, then descended to the ground on gray wings, leaving the doomed inhabitants to either fly to safety or take the slow ride to the forest floor.

"Look . . . they're destroying everything," Iago said in a panic. "You must save me!"

"What about the soldiers who stand behind you, Iago?" Entity303 asked with a wry smile. "What of them?"

"Who cares about them?" Iago screamed in desperation. "You need to save me!"

A few of the soldiers heard this comment and looked back at their king.

"Turn around and defend me against the intruders," Iago commanded. "That is an order!"

The guards looked at each other, apparently confused.

"They aren't very happy to find out they're disposable," Crafter whispered.

"I can see that," Gameknight replied. "Everyone be ready."

The squad leader took a step toward his king. He started at his ruler, expecting Iago to say something.

"I told you to protect me," the king wailed, his emotions now out of control. "DEFEND ME, YOU USELESS KNIGHT!"

The squad leader's posture went from straight and proud to a little slumped. He turned and faced Gameknight999 and the host of cave-dwellers who were still entering the structure, then shook his head. Slowly, he put away his sword, then glanced at his comrades, nodding his head ever so slightly.

"What are you doing? . . . I gave you an order! You are to protect me!" Iago screamed, shaking with disbelief. He turned to Entity303. "Hurry, let me onto your ship before they attack!"

Another soldier put away his sword and stepped aside, followed by three more.

"It seems your army is tired of being sacrificed," the User-that-is-not-a-user said.

Iago glared at Gameknight, then turned to his soldiers.

"Knights, you are to attack them and fight to the last man, or you will all be demoted." Iago was now in a rage, his voice cracking with anger and fear and insanity. "Do you want to fall . . . be one of the fallen? Do you want everyone to know you walk on ground trod upon by the simplest of animals, like those pathetic cave-dwellers?"

More of the soldiers looked back at their king, then put away their swords. The squad leader stepped forward and gave his king one last glare, then reached up, pulled off his ruby-encrusted mask, and threw it to the ground. It shattered into a million pieces.

Gameknight and his friends were shocked to see the face of a zombie underneath, his eyes shining with a silvery light, his face a visage of rage. He stripped off his smock, revealing zombie clothing under chain mail. The zombie knight glared at Iago.

"I am tired of pretending to be the villagers you destroyed so long ago," the soldier growled. "We're zombies, we aren't villagers." The zombie glared at his comrades. "Remove your masks and be your true selves.

The reign of Iago is over. The wars are over. It is now time for peace."

The zombies tore off their masks, threw them aside, then tore off their smocks. They sheathed their swords and stepped aside, allowing the cave-dwellers and villagers to approach.

Just then, the island that held King Iago's massive, multicolored palace groaned like a wounded leviathan, then tipped slightly to its side and began to sink. Everyone turned and watched as the sparkling structure descended to the ground, picking up speed as it fell. Masked zombies leapt from the doomed island, some of them opening their wings and flying away, while others just plummeted downward to their fate.

Entity303 took advantage of the diversion. He kicked Iago in the chest, knocking him backward. The disposed ruler fell hard to the ground, his mask cracking on impact and falling off, revealing his own scarred and decaying zombie face. Entity303 sneered and closed the hatch to the rocket.

"He's gonna take off," Crafter said.

"No, we have to stop him!" Hunter shouted as she fired arrows at the metallic vehicle.

Her arrows bounced harmlessly off the sides of the metal skin. Entity303's smiling face appeared in the window of the rocket, and he waved at Gameknight999 one last time, then blasted off.

"Everyone back up!" Digger shouted.

The stocky NPC grabbed Tux and ran back to the wall of the building. Gameknight moved back as well, but kept his eyes glued to his enemy. The ship slowly crawled up into the air, moving through the huge opening in the roof of the structure, a tail of bright flame blasting from the engines. The ship rose higher and higher into the night sky until it disappeared, the long tongue of fire the only thing marking its existence. And then that too faded, as did Gameknight's hopes.

Entity303 had escaped.

CHAPTER 33

FORPECH

"**H**e's gone," Gameknight moaned. "He was right there . . . we almost had him, but Entity303 escaped."

"Don't worry," Crafter said. "I'm sure you'll think of something."

"ARGHHHH." Iago, the once-ruler, now unmasked zombie, stood with a golden sword in his hands, yelling at the top of his lungs. He pointed his blade at Gameknight999. "You did this. You ruined everything. I'm going to destroy you."

He flourished the weapon around his body like an expert swordsman.

Gameknight could see by the way he handled the blade that he was a lethal adversary.

"Hmmm . . . I think there has been enough violence here," Forpech said his deep voice.

"I'll deal with you later, pech. First, I'm going to destroy Gameknight999. Draw your weapon and prepare to meet your doom," Iago said in a hate-filled voice.

Reaching into his inventory, the User-that-is-not-a-user drew his diamond and iron swords and took a step forward.

"I'm tired of fighting, Iago," Gameknight said. "I just want all this to be over so I can go home."

"You won't be seeing home ever again if I can help it."

The zombie king charged toward Gameknight, but before their swords could meet, a sparkling shaft of light shot through the air and hit Iago square in the chest. It stopped him in his tracks, causing him to drop his sword, his eyes wide with surprise.

"No more fighting, Iago," Forpech grumbled, his deep voice sounding like distant thunder. "You have done great harm here . . . hmmm . . . yes, great harm. But your punishment will not be jail; it will be worse. Your punishment will be to see everything restored as it once was."

The gnome lowered his wand. The green gem at the end of the jagged stick glowed bright, magical energy radiating outward and making the air waver as if overheated. Iago shook his head for a moment, then glared at Gameknight.

"You . . . I'm gonna get you and . . ."

The bright rainbow light shot out of the gnome's wand once again. Forpech advanced with the weapon pointing toward Iago. The energy from the emerald gem seemed to wrap around the king like a multicolored cloak. It then contracted, drawing closer and closer to his skin until it seeped into his flesh, infusing itself with the very fabric of his being.

Iago's scarred face seemed to contort as if he were in agony, but the pain wasn't physical . . . it was something else. His eyes darted about sporadically, looking at the events that were playing through his mind. The expression of shock on his square face slowly morphed to one of disgust, then horror as memories of his past deeds were brought to the forefront of his consciousness.

Slowly, the ruler crumbled to the ground, his arms and legs twitching about in spasms as he writhed in anguish, the colorful light from Forpech's wand now wrapped about him like a new skin. Iago moaned and mumbled things difficult to understand, except for one thing, "I'm sorry . . . I'm so sorry." The apology surfaced many times as the zombie king flailed about, his mind torturing his body.

Gameknight almost felt sorry for the former ruler, but then he thought about all the sorrow he'd caused as a tyrannical dictator. Maybe he deserved this . . . but maybe this kind of suffering was too much? He knew Iago would have killed him if he'd had the chance, but it wasn't in Gameknight's heart to seek revenge. Instead, he felt a sympathetic forgiveness for the ruler and all the terrible things he'd done. Maybe Iago thought he was protecting his people, or maybe he was just insane. But he knew one thing for sure: the path to healing required forgiveness.

The User-that-is-not-a-user glanced at Weaver. The young boy had a horrified look on his face as he watched the zombie king suffering. Gameknight knew he felt some of what Iago was experiencing when he thought about Weaver. He'd failed at protecting him at the end of the Great Zombie Invasion, and now he had to keep things from him to avoid telling him too much about the future. Weaver was angry at being left out and Gameknight understood that. He hoped the boy could someday forgive him. But as he watched Iago struggle with his past deeds, Gameknight realized he had to do the same. He had done his best to protect all those villagers in the past, and he was doing his best now. Instead of hanging onto what he'd failed at, he instead accepted his weaknesses and forgave himself.

It was as if a gigantic weight had been lifted from his body. He stood up tall for the first time in what seemed like forever. When he glanced back at Weaver, he found the boy smiling at him, the angry light of resentment in the NPC's blue eyes faded to that of understanding and forgiveness. The villager nodded, and Gameknight returned it with a nod of his own, a smile growing on his face.

Finally, Forpech lowered his wand, the light from the magical weapon extinguished.

Iago lay there for a moment, not moving, then opened his eyes and looked up at the pech. Slowly, he stood, checking his body for injuries . . . but the pain had only been psychological, from within his mind.

Glancing around, Iago saw all eyes upon him, faces of anger and contempt and resentment all focused on him, rightfully so. And as he glanced from one accuser to the next, the great king finally broke down and wept. He sobbed until there were no more tears left to shed, then raised his head and peered up at Forpech.

"Third, you have taught me much," Iago said sadly. He wiped square tears from his eyes.

Forpech nodded, his dark eyes seemingly filled with sympathy for the zombie king.

"I understand what I have done and how I have hurt so many," Iago said. He turned and looked at his guards, their black smocks and shattered white masks lying at their feet. "I can only hope you will all forgive me. I was so wrong to put you in harm's way just to satisfy my greed."

He turned to Thorin and Thea, who had moved to Gameknight's side.

"And I did terrible things to your people." Iago stepped forward and knelt before the two hulking cave-dwellers. "I can only hope you can forgive me as the zombie people strive to make things right."

"What's going on?" Hunter asked. "Forpech, what did your wand do to him?"

"Hmmm . . . my wand forces the target and the wielder to face themselves and accept themselves for who they truly are. A person can never be forgiven by another until they first forgive themselves. My wand . . . hmmm . . . forced Iago to confront what he has done to others and feel their pain so that then he can be worthy of their forgiveness. He has accepted his responsibility for these atrocities and has begun the difficult task of forgiving himself. Now he must earn the forgiveness of the ones he's wronged. Iago will never be at peace until all of them truly forgive him. Hmmm . . . until then, he will strive to serve everyone he has harmed."

"That might end up being quite the harsh punishment," Crafter said.

"Forgiveness is a tricky thing, yes, yes," Empech said. "It can be difficult to give to another," the gnome glanced at Weaver, then looked pointedly toward Gameknight999, "but is even more difficult to give to oneself, yes, yes."

Weaver turned toward the User-that-is-not-a-user, tears seeping from his blue eyes. "I'm sorry I was so mad at you about, you know," the young boy said. "I'm sure you were just trying to protect everyone—no, to protect Minecraft itself—by pretending to be Smithy."

"I'm sorry I couldn't tell you," Gameknight replied, "and even now there are things I cannot tell you, because . . ."

"I know, the timeline must be protected from any changes," Weaver said.

The young boy moved to Gameknight and gave him a huge hug, then turned and faced Herder.

"And I know I said it earlier, but I'm sorry for taking my frustration and jealousy out on you, Herder. I know Gameknight can be friends with you and me. I just had a hard time understanding that."

"Gameknight frequently makes things complicated," Hunter added with a sarcastic smile.

"This is all great," Digger said, his booming voice echoing off the stone walls, "but what do we do about Entity303?"

Suddenly, Kahn landed on the ground next to Gameknight, Deimos held under one arm. The huge fire demon folded in his dark wings then set the little fire-imp on the ground. The zombies drew their swords as if getting ready for battle, but Gameknight held up his hands, motioning for them to lower their blades.

"I seee your preyyy escaped," the demon said. "He flees to the starrrs?"

"Apparently so," the User-that-is-not-a-user replied. "But what Entity303 doesn't understand is I know a lot about the mod he just used. It's called Galacticraft, and it lets users go to other planets in Minecraft's outer space using rocket ships. I know how this mod works and how to use it to our advantage." He turned to face his friends. "We're gonna build a spaceship of our own and pursue him."

"Yeah!" Hunter exclaimed.

"But the ship seemed to only hold one passenger," Crafter said.

"Yeah, I know. I haven't figured out how to get all of us up there into space yet."

"I havvve a solllution." Kahn reached into his inventory and produced two rings. He gave one to Gameknight999, and the other he tossed to Crafter. "These arrre teleportation ringgggs. They willll allow onnne to teleport to the otherrrr."

"That's perfect," Gameknight exclaimed.

Crafter looked confused.

"Look, we can build a rocket and I can get up there into space," the User-that-is-not-a-user explained. "When I get everything set up, I'll teleport the rest of you to me. Then we can continue the chase."

"I like this idea," Hunter said. "Going into space where there's no air, landing on an alien planet that probably has alien monsters. This sounds like one of your best plans yet!"

"Don't worry, I know what I'm doing," Gameknight said.

"That's what you said when we faced the Ender Dragon, and when we faced the Elder Guardian, and the four horsemen, and the zombie king, and the blaze king, and the Lich King . . . and let's not forget the Hydra. It seems like you always say that," she replied with a knowing smile.

Gameknight just shrugged, then moved to the chests that lined one of the walls and began looking for what he needed.

CHAPTER 34

TO THE STARS

Everyone watched Gameknight999 as if he were a madman.

He ran from chest to chest, pulling out huge chunks of metal plating and large rocket parts. King Iago ran at his side, helping out wherever possible.

"When Entity303 had us build these things for him, I figured it would be useful to make a couple of extras," the king explained. "I'm sure there are enough parts for another rocket."

"What about fuel?" Gameknight asked, looking around.

"That's one thing we have a lot of," the zombie king explained. "Our oil wells are still feeding into the refineries. There will be ample rocket fuel for the ship. We also have the oxygen generators working at full speed. The oxygen tanks will be filled in no time."

Gameknight nodded, then cast a glance to the east. The black sun was showing its dark face from behind the horizon. The sparkling stars slowly faded as the sky turned from black to a deep red, to orange, yellow, and then its usual pale green. Across the world, huge empty spaces separated some of the sky islands. A great number had been sent downward, their levitation blocks destroyed to the point where the glowing cubes could no longer support the weight of the land. Those that now lay on the forest floor were being torn apart by the Mogs and Glugs, their red grass being replanted throughout the forest.

All across the remaining sky islands, cave-dwellers were taking control of the surviving soldiers, ushering them down to the treetops, then flying to the next islands to make sure all of the zombies had been disarmed.

There were still skirmishes, with groups of zombies wanting to hold onto their place above the rest of the creatures in this world. But it was easy enough to convince most of the sky-dwellers to surrender.

As he worked, Gameknight ignored the commotion around him. Crafter was trying to organize the cave-dwellers into some kind of government, hoping to avoid any reprisals for past misdeeds by the sky-dwellers. But the User-that-is-not-a-user paid them no heed. All he wanted to do was catch Entity303 before he did any more damage, and get Weaver back where he belonged. And to do that, they needed that terrible user to tell them where the portal was hidden that would lead back into Minecraft's past.

As the dark sun climbed into the sky, the rocket ship took shape, growing taller and taller. Finally, with a satisfied smile, he was finished.

"Is it done?" Stitcher asked.

Gameknight nodded his head, then wiped his sweaty brow. He gathered his companions.

"Here's the plan. I'm going up in the rocket. When I get there, I'll get everything set up, then I'll use the teleportation ring from Kahn and bring the rest of you to me." He glanced at Iago. "They all need oxygen gear, helmets, and O^2 tanks."

"They'll be ready," Iago promised.

"I don't think going up there alone is a good idea," Hunter said. "That seems kinda dangerous. You need another set of eyes with you to watch your back."

"I know, but the rocket will only hold one person."

Squawk! Tux suddenly demanded.

"Tux, I can't take you with me; it'll be dangerous."

Squawk, squawk!

Gameknight looked at Digger, hoping for some help with the little animal. The stocky NPC just shrugged his muscular shoulders. The penguin waddled forward and pecked at Gameknight's leg, her bright yellow beak making a pinging sound as it bounced off his diamond leggings.

"Seems like you're gonna have a passenger whether you like it or not," Digger said with a smile.

"I can't take her," Gameknight objected. "She'd need oxygen gear and a space helmet and . . ."

"Not to worry, the equipment my engineers made will fit anyone," Iago said.

He stepped forward and put the square transparent helmet on the animal's head, then strapped the oxygen tanks to the penguin's back. They both shrunk to fit the tiny animal's size. Instantly, Tux was transformed from a mere penguin to a space-penguin.

SQUAWK, SQUAWK! the penguin said, her voice muffled by the space helmet.

Gameknight sighed with resignation, then nodded his head and put on his own helmet before donning his oxygen gear and tanks.

"Wait," Iago said, then rushed to another chest.

The zombie pulled something out that glowed bright yellow. When he turned, Iago held a blazing yellow sword in his green hands, the handle decorated with bright red gems. Hunter instantly pulled out her bow and notched an arrow, suspicious and ready to fire.

Iago ignored her and turned the sword around. He extended it to Gameknight999, handle first.

"This is the same as Entity303's sword," the zombie explained. "It is an infused sword, fully charged with energy. Maybe this will give you a small edge when you finally face that evil user."

"I hope so," Gameknight said as he reached out and took the weapon. "Thank you."

King Iago nodded and stepped back.

"Well, I guess this is it," the User-that-is-not-a-user said.

He scanned the faces of his friends. Each bore an expression of concern, and to be fair, his own face probably looked the same.

"You don't need to worry. I've done this dozens of times."

"But not when you were actually *in* Minecraft," Hunter said. "This is different and you know it."

Gameknight said nothing; she was right.

"Just be careful," she added, then smiled. "And don't be an idiot."

"I'll try not to." He glanced down at the penguin. "Tux, you ready?"

Squaaawk! the penguin said, her screechy voice sounding impatient.

"Then get in, Tux, and let's do this."

The penguin jumped up and down, then scurried into the rocket. Gameknight followed the animal, stepping up to the metallic ship. Inside, it was cramped, with lights blinking and a control panel covered with levers and buttons.

The door slammed with an ominous clank. The User-that-is-not-a-user looked through the glass at his friends. Hunter yelled something to him, but he couldn't hear through the ship's hull. Waving to his comrades, he pressed the launch button.

The ship began to rumble. It was at first a gentle sound, like thunder from a distant storm. But then it grew in volume until the walls of the ship were shaking and the noise made it nearly impossible to hear his own thoughts. Rising into the air, Gameknight watched through the window as his friends grew smaller and smaller. Soon, he could only see the cobblestone structure that sat on the sky island. And then the sky islands shrunk as he went higher and higher into the air. Finally, the terrible green sky was pulled back, revealing the blackness of space as they pierced the thin veil of atmosphere that surrounded the world. Sparkling stars surrounded the ship as it continued to shudder and vibrate, the roaring engines enveloping everything.

Below them now was the blue, green, and white cube that was Minecraft, the digital world floating there with the immensity of space extending out in all directions.

Gameknight looked down at Tux.

"Well, Tux, I guess there's no turning back now."

Squawk, the animal replied, her high-pitched voice barely audible.

"Yeah, I'm nervous too, but soon this space flight will be over, and we'll be on the moon."

Gameknight stared out the window into the endless depths of outer space. Images of all the villagers and creatures who had suffered because of his enemy appeared in his mind, causing rage to boil up from the deepest recesses of his soul. He grew angrier and angrier as he thought about all the pain Entity303 had caused, just because he'd been fired by the Minecraft programming team. His fury grew so great Gameknight had to let it out, somehow.

"You've called down the thunder and now you got it," he shouted and shook his fist. "There is no place you can go where I can't find you. Not even the deepest, darkest places in outer space will hide you from me. I'm coming for you, Entity303!"

Squawk squawk! Tux added.

Gameknight looked down at his friend and patted her on top of her little helmet, then glared at the sparkling stars and waited for them to reach the moon.

MINECRAFT SEEDS

Sadly, I don't have any Minecraft seeds for you, as the worlds that are generated in Mystcraft can only be seen from within the Mystcraft mod. I've attached a list of some videos on YouTube that show some examples of some really cool stuff on Mystcraft. I prefer to watch the mod videos from Direwolf20, and his channel is here: https://www.youtube.com/user/direwolf20. His videos are very informative, and he always uses appropriate language for kids, so go check out his stuff.

DireWolf20 made a great mod showcase video that goes through many of the features in Mystcraft. You can find that video here: https://youtu.be/sNSkjEvB_f8.

He created a fantastic video to teach you how to write your own Ages in Mystcraft. When you try this, you should not get discouraged; writing Ages is challenging and takes practice. Watch his video, and take notes so when you do it, hopefully you'll get what you're trying to create. There are a number of other Mystcraft Age Writing tutorials on YouTube. If you don't like Direwolf20's tutorial, go check out some of the others, but here's his tutorial: https://youtu.be/-V_YENljUao.

Here is a video of DireWolf20 exploring some Ages and showing how to navigate through the different Ages you can create. Don't forget to bring a linking book so you can get back to the Overworld: https://youtu.be/ IMR60yRQmo0.

To load Mystcraft, I found it easier to either download Feed-the-Beast, https://www.feed-the-beast.com/, and then use the DireWolf20 modpack, which worked really well on my macbook (be sure to get your parent's permission before downloading anything), but you can also download the Curse Client, https://mods.curse.com/ client, which is another way to run modded Minecraft. Here is a video with DireWolf20 showing how to use the newer Curse Client: https://youtu.be/lf2y1D8w-MdU. Be aware, running modded Minecraft takes a lot of resources on your computer. On my PC, I can't run either the Curse Client or Feed-the-Beast, because it just gets too laggy; my PC is too old. But they will run on my Macbook, which is much newer and has more horsepower. So you may run into issues if you try these. Please be sure to ask your parents' permission before downloading anything.

Modded Minecraft is fantastic, and there are incredible mods out there like Twilight Forest, or Galacticraft (Minecraft in space), but be careful what you are downloading. These things are free, and you should never be required to purchase anything to use these.

Good luck with your Ages, and don't forget your linking book!

AVAILABLE NOW FROM MARK CHEVERTON AND SKY PONY PRESS

THE GAMEKNIGHT999 SERIES
The world of Minecraft comes to life in this thrilling adventure!

Gameknight999 loved Minecraft, and above all else, he loved to grief—to intentionally ruin the gaming experience for other users.

But when one of his father's inventions teleports him into the game, Gameknight is forced to live out a real-life adventure inside a digital world. What will happen if he's killed? Will he respawn? Die in real life? Stuck in the game, Gameknight discovers Minecraft's best-kept secret, something not even the game's programmers realize: the creatures within the game are alive! He will have to stay one step ahead of the sharp claws of zombies and pointed fangs of spiders, but he'll also have to learn to make friends and work as a team if he has any chance of surviving the Minecraft war his arrival has started.

With deadly Endermen, ghasts, and dragons, this action-packed trilogy introduces the heroic Gameknight999 and has proven to be a runaway publishing smash, showing that the Gameknight999 series is the perfect companion for Minecraft fans of all ages.

Invasion of the Overworld (Book One):
$9.99 paperback • 978-1-63220-711-1

Battle for the Nether (Book Two):
$9.99 paperback • 978-1-63220-712-8

Confronting the Dragon (Book Three):
$9.99 paperback • 978-1-63450-046-3

AVAILABLE NOW FROM MARK CHEVERTON AND SKY PONY PRESS

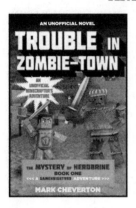

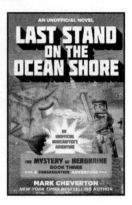

THE MYSTERY OF HEROBRINE SERIES
Gameknight999 must save his friends from an evil virus intent on destroying all of Minecraft!

Gameknight999 was sucked into the world of Minecraft when one of his father's inventions went haywire. Trapped inside the game, the former griefer learned the error of his ways, transforming into a heroic warrior and defeating powerful Endermen, ghasts, and dragons to save the world of Minecraft and his NPC friends who live in it.

Gameknight swore he'd never go inside Minecraft again. But that was before Herobrine, a malicious virus infecting the very fabric of the game, threatened to destroy the entire Overworld and escape into the real world. To outsmart an enemy much more powerful than any he's ever faced, the User-that-is-not-a-user will need to go back into the game, where real danger lies around every corner. From zombie villages and jungle temples to a secret hidden at the bottom of a deep ocean, the action-packed adventures of Gameknight999 and his friends (and, now, family) continue in this thrilling follow-up series for Minecraft fans of all ages.

Trouble in Zombie-town (Book One):
$9.99 paperback • 978-1-63450-094-4

The Jungle Temple Oracle (Book Two):
$9.99 paperback • 978-1-63450-096-8

Last Stand on the Ocean Shore (Book Three):
$9.99 paperback • 978-1-63450-098-2

AVAILABLE NOW FROM MARK CHEVERTON AND SKY PONY PRESS

HEROBRINE REBORN SERIES
Gameknight999 and his friends and family face Herobrine in the biggest showdown the Overworld has ever seen!

Gameknight999, a former Minecraft griefer, got a big dose of virtual reality when his father's invention teleported him into the game. Living out a dangerous adventure inside a digital world, he discovered that the Minecraft villagers were alive and needed his help to defeat the infamous virus, Herobrine, a diabolical enemy determined to escape into the real world.

Gameknight thought Herobrine had finally been stopped once and for all. But the virus proves to be even craftier than anyone could imagine, and his XP begins inhabiting new bodies in an effort to escape. The User-that-is-not-a-user will need the help of not only his Minecraft friends, but his own father, Monkeypants271, as well, if he has any hope of destroying the evil Herobrine once and for all.

Saving Crafter (Book One):
$9.99 paperback • 978-1-5107-0014-7

Destruction of the Overworld (Book Two):
$9.99 paperback • 978-1-5107-0015-4

Gameknight999 vs. Herobrine (Book Three):
$9.99 paperback • 978-1-5107-0010-9

  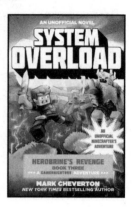

AVAILABLE NOW FROM MARK CHEVERTON
AND SKY PONY PRESS

THE BIRTH OF HEROBRINE SERIES
Can Gameknight999 survive a journey one hundred years into Minecraft's past?

A freak thunderstorm strikes just as Gameknight999 is activating his father's digitizer to re-enter Minecraft. Sparks flash across his vision as he is sucked into the game . . . and when the smoke clears he's arrived safely. But it doesn't take long to realize that things in the Overworld are very different.

The User-that-is-not-a-user realizes he's been accidentally sent a hundred years into the past, back to the time of the historic Great Zombie Invasion. None of his friends have even been born yet. But that might be the least of Gameknight999's worries, because travelling back in time also means that the evil virus Herobrine, the scourge of Minecraft, is still alive . . .

The Great Zombie Invasion (Book One):
$9.99 paperback • 978-1-5107-0994-2

Attack of the Shadow-crafters (Book Two):
$9.99 paperback • 978-1-5107-0995-9

Herobrine's War (Book Three):
$9.99 paperback • 978-1-5107-0996-7

EXCERPT FROM MISSION TO THE MOON

A BRAND NEW GAMEKNIGHT999 ADVENTURE

Gameknight landed in a large room devoid of any noise. The silence was spooky . . . almost oppressive, making it seem as if a monster horde could jump out of the darkness at any instant. His breathing seemed amplified inside his helmet, the wheezy in and out being performed to the drum beat of his quickening heart. His nerves tingled as he waited for claws to reach out at him or arrows to streak through the thin Martian air . . . but the attack never came.

Forpech and Empech put glowstone torches on the walls, revealing a chamber lined with green bricks. Blocks of spider web clung to the walls and ceiling, but no fuzzy black monsters, with their eight terrible green eyes, were visible.

"Where are the monsters?" Gameknight asked softly. The silence made him want to be as quiet as possible.

"Are you complaining?" Hunter whispered.

"No, I just don't like surprises, and no monsters waiting for us is a surprise."

"The monster spawners have been removed, yes, yes," Empech said, his high-pitched, screechy voice echoing off the brick walls. The volume of it, though at a normal speaking level, was shocking as it sliced through the stillness.

"One's been removed over here as well," Digger added from off to the side.

"Why would Entity303 take away the spawners?" Weaver asked. "That makes no sense. He could have just destroyed the monsters that were here and then left before any more creatures appeared."

"Maybe he's worried for our safety," Hunter said with a chuckle.

"Yeah, I'm sure that's it," Weaver agreed with a wry smile.

"I think it's safe to say, Entity303 didn't destroy the spawners to make it easy on us," Crafter said. "We all know that's not his way. He'd rather we suffered as much as possible, and destroying the spawners is the opposite."

"Hmmm . . . we must proceed with caution, yes, yes" Empech said. "Expect the unexpected and be ready, that is Empech's advice."

"Thanks for stating the obvious," Hunter said.

Stitcher punched her in the arm.

"Ouch . . . you keep hitting me in the same spot."

"That's because you keep saying dumb things," the younger sister replied.

"We must continue on," Forpech grumbled, his deep voice making the walls of the dungeon vibrate just a bit. "Hmmm . . . we must find the Mars Boss and determine what he knows about our enemy, Entity303."

"Right." Gameknight drew his steeleaf shield and held it before him, enchanted diamond sword also at the ready. Waves of iridescent light flowed from the weapon, painting the walls with a faint purple glow, but not enough light to really see anything in the passage. "Weaver, up front with me. We need to place glowstone torches as we go." He glanced over his shoulder. "Digger, you collect the torches as we move through the dungeon, so we won't run out."

The big NPC nodded, then scooped Tux up with his left hand, his big pickaxe in his right.

"Come on, everyone."

Gameknight moved through the dark passage, scanning the ground for pressure plates, trip wires or holes. It would be just like Entity303 to leave behind some traps. They moved through the tunnel in complete silence, only the sounds of their footsteps echoing off the walls. The lack of any other noise made everything around them seem so much louder: the clank of iron armor, the scrape of a sword against the wall, the sound of a glowstone torch being broken. The silence in the dungeon was almost deafening, stretching their nerves to the limit.

The passage led to another chamber. And as before, it had been swept clean of monsters and spawners. The only evidence anything had ever been there was the two holes in the ground where the spawners had once been placed.

Water dripped from overhead. The sound of the splashing droplet on the ground made Gameknight jump.

"What was that?" Digger asked.

"Water from the ceiling," Gameknight replied.

"Why is there water up there?" Stitcher asked. "I didn't see any lakes or rivers on the surface."

Gameknight shrugged. "It's just the way some of these dungeons are programmed. They've always been this way."

"Well, I don't like it," Hunter said.

"I'll let Micdoodle8, the developer of GalactiCraft, know that . . . if I ever see him," Gameknight replied with a smirk.

"Wait, that was sarcastic, but you didn't punch him," Hunter complained to her younger sister.

"His sarcastic comments are at least funny," Stitcher replied with a smile.

"Funny . . . you call that funny?"

Stitcher punched her sibling lightly in the arm, then laughed.

"Come on," Gameknight said. "Let's get to the next chamber."

They moved quickly through the dungeon, the green bricks that lined the walls and floors creating an eerie look in the light of the glowstone torches. The occasional splatter of water drops from the ceiling continued, each drip sounding like a thunderous deluge in the empty silence. Gameknight's heart thumped in his chest, pounding faster and faster as they moved through the dungeon. When they reached the next chamber, Gameknight charged in, ready for a monstrous response. But like the first, this room was completely devoid of monsters, the spawners destroyed.

"This is gonna be easy," Hunter said.

"Shhh . . . you're gonna jinx it," Weaver said.

"Pffft, no big deal," she added.

"Come on, let's keep moving," Gameknight said as he dashed through the chamber and through the dark passage.

They passed through more empty chambers, each like the last.

"I don't like this," Crafter said after going through yet another vacant room. "Entity303 would never do something that might make it easier for us."

"I agree," said the User-that-is-not-a-user, "but let's just keep moving."

They ran through the passage, turning to the left and right, then entered another room that seemed larger than the rest, the walls shrouded in darkness. Again, there were no monsters visible. They moved through the chamber and headed into the next corridor, Gameknight and Weaver leading, Digger and Crafter bringing up the rear.

Suddenly, the User-that-is-not-a-user skidded to a stop. A huge wall of cobblestone blocked off the tunnel, stretching from floor to ceiling.

"What is this?" Weaver asked.

"I don't think this is supposed to be here," Gameknight said. "Likely Entity303 built it."

"But what is he trying to keep us from?" Herder asked.

"Perhaps the wall was not meant to keep us out," Forpech said. "Hmmm . . . but instead meant to just keep us here."

"But why would that annoying user want to just stop us here? He knows we could just dig through this obstacle," Gameknight said.

He glanced at Digger. The stocky NPC placed Tux on the ground and moved to the wall. With a gigantic swing, he smashed his pickaxe into the cobblestone. Cracks spread across the face as he tore into the cube until finally it broke. But behind it was another block. Digger carved into that block as well until it disappeared, revealing another block of cobblestone behind that.

"Hmmm . . . perhaps there is more to this wall than meets the eye," Forpech said.

Squawk, squawk! Tux suddenly screamed from the back of the passage.

"Tux, be quiet; we need to figure this out," Gameknight chided.

Squawk, squawk, squawk.

"What is wrong with that penguin?" Hunter said as she peered into the hole Digger had carved.

Suddenly, a moan filled the passage. It caused Gameknight to freeze as fingers of dread clawed into his soul, making him shiver. A clicking accompanied the sorrowful wails, followed by the clattering of bones.

"I don't think we're alone in here," Crafter said in a soft voice.

"You think?" Hunter asked.

Stitcher punched her sister in the arm, then drew her bow and notched an arrow. Herder ran down the length of the passage and placed a glowstone torch on the ground, then retreated. As they watched, zombies in glowing armor, complete with space helmets and oxygen tanks, moved into the light, followed by spiders and skeletons, their eyes all glaring at the intruders.

"We have no way out," Digger moaned, his voice cracking with fear. He hacked away at the cobblestone wall, but found layer after layer of stone.

"It seems we have few choices, yes, yes," Empech said.

The little gray gnome moved away from the monsters and backed against the cobblestone wall.

"I won't let a bunch of monsters slow us down." Gameknight glanced at Digger. "Get to work on this wall. We need a way through as quickly as possible."

"What are you going to do?" Crafter asked.

"The only thing I'm good for," Gameknight replied.

He tossed his shield to Empech, then drew his iron sword. Turning, the User-that-is-not-a-user faced the approaching mob, then yelled with all his might as he charged, "FOR MINECRAFT!"

COMING SOON:
MISSION TO THE MOON
THE MYSTERY OF ENTITY303 BOOK THREE